Dog-Tired

CHRISTMAS

Lori Hayes

Library of Congress Control Number: Applied For

Published in the United States by Seaquine Publishing

Website: LoriHayesAuthor.com

ISBN: 979-8-9871000-3-5

MORE BOOKS BY LORI HAYES

CRYSTAL COAST SERIES

HIGH TIDE
COFFEE BREAK
ISLAND SUMMER
COASTAL CHRISTMAS

STAND-ALONE NOVELS
SAVING NEVADA
DOG-TIRED CHRISTMAS

KIDS' BOOKS
WRITING AS LISA MORGAN

THE CHRISTMAS HORSE
TROUBLED HEARTS
MYSTERY HORSE
RUNNING WILD
TRAIL TROUBLE

DEDICATION

After I wrote Dog-Tired Christmas, Tropical Storm Helene devastated western North Carolina and surrounding areas. My heart goes out to all of you! I questioned my editor if I should release this book because of the unfortunate timing, but she suggested that we go ahead, as so many people need hope. All of you are in my prayers. Stay safe.

CHAPTER ONE

Owning an antique store was my dream come true. Well, except for dealing with cranky customers who forgot their morning dose of caffeine. Today proved to be one of those challenging days.

The bell above the door chimed and my mother breezed in like a welcomed ray of golden sunshine on a rainy fall day. Her flowy, burnt-orange dress made her seem so carefree.

Smiling at her, my exhaustion slipped away. "Be with you in a minute, Mom."

"Take your time, sweetheart." She browsed the store like usual, searching for new items on the shelves along the wall.

I walked around the counter to ring up a customer who bought a Delft bowl. "Would you like the dish wrapped?" The woman nodded, and I got busy creating a beautiful gift with red paper and curly silver ribbon. When I handed her the elegant package she swooned and left the store.

My cell phone sang an upbeat Christmas tune, despite the month having barely slid into November. I normally didn't answer with customers in the store, but my cousin's name flashed on the screen, and she never video chatted during work hours. An emergency?

I inhaled a slow breath to stay calm before I answered, but when the video popped on, a handsome man stared back at me. Ashley hadn't mentioned dating anyone so I grew more concerned.

"I'm Chris, a friend of Ashley's. You must be Brittany." He paused, glancing behind him at someone appearing lifeless on a hospital bed. "I have some bad news."

My breath caught and I tried to fight off tears. Was that Ashley? The poor lighting made it difficult to tell.

Mom rushed to the counter beside me. She leaned in closer to the screen and gasped. "Oh my gosh, what happened?"

"Ashley had a little accident." Chris's brows drew in a concerned line across his forehead, and he rubbed a nervous hand across his trimmed beard. "She missed a couple of steps at home when hurrying to get ready for work on time. Her neighbor didn't answer the phone when she called for help, so she reached out to me. I insisted she go to the emergency department."

My hand shot to my mouth.

"She'll be okay, but the doctor said she broke her shoulder in three places and will possibly need surgery. She has an appointment with the surgeon on Tuesday." He paused as if to keep his composure and continued. "The biggest problem is her intense pain, but they'll be sending her home with a sling for now. She mentioned you might be willing to come to town to help?"

I paused to absorb all he'd said. "To help?"

His deep, rich voice lowered. "Yes, for a few weeks."

I felt bad for her, but how could I step away from my shop during the holiday rush to head to the mountains? Mom flashed me a look of concern.

"Think about it, but please let me know today if you can."

I agreed and we ended the call. My emotions danced in circles, ranging from guilt if I didn't go to worrying about my business if I did.

Mom reached across the counter to help herself to a chocolate chip cookie made by Sugar Pastries, the bakery across the street from me. They'd been delivering the best treats to us since I opened Time-Worn Treasures.

"These are delicious. Nothing better than a cookie to ward off stress." She smacked her lips and brushed the crumbs from her dress and onto the floor. Dusting off her fingers, she pulled out a couple of pamphlets from her purse.

She had never been a tidy housekeeper, and I figured I inherited the "neat" trait from my father.

"This might be a good time to announce our news in case it helps you decide about going to the mountains. Poor Ashley." She frowned. "Guess where your dad and I are going for the holidays?"

I glanced up, biting my lower lip. It took everything I had not to offend her by pulling out the vacuum.

She didn't seem to notice my reaction and fanned the pamphlets out on the counter for me to admire. A colorful photo of a river boat attracted my attention instantly along with a festive Christmas market.

"We'll be gone for Thanksgiving, Christmas, and New Year's." I swore her entire face smiled.

I picked up one of the brochures, trying my best to keep an open mind about possibly being alone for the holidays. "This trip looks amazing, but why Christmas?"

If I had to pick a favorite holiday to stay home for, Christmas won several times over.

There was nothing better than hunkering down in my small beach town during the holidays with family, friends, and food, where life was safe, cozy, and familiar.

She shrugged. "Why not?

"Christmas won't be the same without you both. You always invite everyone over on Christmas Eve." Those who didn't have plans or family nearby gravitated to our house for a meal and community. Holidays were meant to be spent with family and friends. I loved living in the small beach town of Seaview, North Carolina, where everyone knew each other and I could make trips to the beach whenever I wanted, even during winter.

When it came to decorating, the town barred no limits. The committee took pride in encircling black ornate lamp posts with green garland and illuminated shells, seahorses, and sailboats. Every year Seaport held a quaint Christmas parade a week before the holiday with handmade floats, old-time cars, and a firetruck with Santa riding on top while tossing candy to the kids.

No matter how exciting the trip to Europe sounded, why would my parents want to leave all that behind?

Mom answered as if reading my mind. "This trip has been a dream of ours. We'll also spend time traveling around on our own, staying in different towns."

"Sounds exciting." I thumbed through the brochures, mesmerized by the photos on the ads. "Mom, what a spectacular opportunity." My parents deserved to ring in their early retirement with a trip of a lifetime.

She placed her hand on mine. "Just imagine seeing all the charming Christmas markets."

"You sound like a marketing brochure," I said, marveling at the idea of my mom and dad taking such a vacation. Maybe someday I would too. "It will be good for you both. Together time."

My best friend Nancy Baker walked into the store and wandered toward us, checking out the few new items along the way. I always admired her silky blonde hair and flowy bohemian style dresses made of natural fibers like cotton or linen.

Mom switched the topic back to Ashley. "Are you going to head up to Snow Valley?"

Nancy looked at us with interest. "Why would you go to the mountains?"

"Because Ashley fell and broke her arm in three places." My mom loved to gossip.

I sighed. "I want to help her but it's almost impossible to leave the store, especially during holidays."

Nancy waved her arms in the air. "I can help," she said with excitement. She had been out of work for a month, but she didn't know antiques, nor how to run a store. Then again, she did excel as a corporate management assistant. Unfortunately, her previous employer initiated heavy layoffs and eliminated her job.

"I appreciate the offer." I inhaled a long breath to try to relax. "How about I call you tonight after I have a chance to process the details?"

"Sounds fair enough. You can always coach me while you're in the mountains. It's been ten years, but I worked retail while I attended college." Nancy talked fast, using her hands for emphasis. Perhaps she wanted to get out of the house and work, or maybe she needed holiday money as well.

Mom placed her hand on mine. "Family needs you. What choice do you have?"

She was right; family came first. What to do? "I'll let you know what I come up with."

Mom scooped up the pamphlets and shoved them into her purse. "The Great Smoky Mountains might be a peaceful respite for you. Goodness knows, dear, you deserve a vacation."

True. I couldn't remember the last time I had a week off, much less several. Besides, I wasn't thrilled about spending the holidays alone at home.

I spent the rest of the day helping an endless flow of customers, my feet throbbing. Chris popped into my mind several times after the video chat, his deep, sexy voice and gentle eyes enticing me.

Right before closing time, Mr. Holmes entered for the second time today, finally deciding to buy a valuable Louis Comfort Tiffany lamp. It hurt a little to sell such a gorgeous piece, but holding onto all the treasures for myself wasn't a smart business strategy.

Once the day ended, I stopped by my favorite restaurant to grab a takeout order of chicken wings and fries before heading home. The rest of the night I recovered on my comfy couch with my feet elevated on the coffee table, contemplating the trip to the mountains. I couldn't help but think of Chris again, so I searched Ashley's social media but didn't find him on her friends' list, surprising me. I did know a few guys who didn't have an online presence but it wasn't the norm.

I wished my favorite and only cousin had the ability to come here to heal. Truth be told, I had only driven to the mountains to visit her once for a brief weekend. Lately, even catching up on the phone proved difficult with our demanding lifestyles. But staying connected to her remained important to me.

When we were young, I pretended she was my sister. We played together as kids, spending nights at each other's houses whenever possible, wearing matching clothes and telling people we were twins, although no one believed us.

Ashley had moved to Snow Valley, North Carolina, after she finished college at East Carolina University with a Bachelor of Arts degree in Communication. Even though I had only visited Snow Valley once, the quaint town left a positive impression on me. I adored how the town was nestled by the mountains. Ashley loved snow, but I loved sand.

Wanting more details now that my belly was full, I dialed Ashley's number, half expecting Mr. Sexy to answer again. Unfortunately, he did not.

"How are you feeling?" I asked when she answered with a strained voice.

"Horrible. It's hurts to the point I can't move without crying."

I winced at the thought. "My poor cuz. Do you think you'll need surgery?" If so, I needed to drive up there to help her immediately.

"Ohhhh!" A muffled shuffling commotion sounded over the phone, sobbing.

"Ashley?"

Another muted noise came through the earpiece. "Oh, my gosh," she said with a jagged breath. "I dropped the phone and when I reached down to grab it, a sharp pain ripped through my arm."

"Are you home alone, or is Chris there with you?" I wondered if they were dating or just friends.

"I'm alone, and I need help. If I ask my mom, she's guaranteed to drive me nuts. Besides, she doesn't like to drive from the beach up here alone, so I can't ask her." Ashley's parents divorced when we were in high school, and Ashley didn't have a close relationship with her dad. Her mom had moved two hours south of me. "Jill just moved to California, and lately my sister and I don't get along all that well. Besides, she has young kids." Ashley let out a sharp squeal into the phone. "I can't move, can't sleep, can't even pull up my own pants after using the restroom. Will you come to the mountains to help me? Please."

A wave of guilt washed through me. "I'd like to, but I have to figure out the logistics." The idea overwhelmed me. Maybe Nancy would be fine to run my store, but business usually picked up the closer we got to the holidays.

"Can you do me a favor if you do come up here?" Ashley asked suddenly. "Our event planner at work quit, and right before I fell, my new boss assigned me to organize the Christmas Candlelight Home Tour."

"I know next to nothing about planning events." I mean, I believed in helping family however needed, but antiques were my line of expertise. Not event planning.

"Understandable. First, I need to rummage through a large box of miscellaneous items to see where Claire, the one who quit, left off. Social media and marketing are my specialty more than arranging events."

"Do you have vacation time you can take?" If I drove up there, I wanted to help Ashley get settled as soon as possible. A quick and easy trip, and I'd be back home in no time.

She screeched again. In a strained voice she whispered, "Sorry, I tried to get more comfortable on the couch. I don't have the mind space to plan the event right now … so I'd be happy to share my pay with you."

I shook my head. "No way, but we'll have to discuss the event in more detail later if I come."

"Please drive up here and stay for a few weeks. I need your help and can't do this without you."

I tended to want to please people despite the havoc it caused in my own life. Her words made me feel guilty.

How could I say no?

Chris Hart opened the back door of his restaurant to drag two bags of trash to the dumpster. A filthy black Labrador Retriever mix had his front paws on its rim, sniffing the air to catch a whiff of leftover food from last night's special—ribs drenched in a savory red sauce.

"Hey there, boy. Haven't you eaten?" The dog glanced up at him with curious eyes. "You're a nice pup and must belong to someone. I bet they're looking for you."

The dog didn't wear a collar, but he wagged his tail at Chris's words. He whined, his paws still on the dumpster.

"Let's see what food I can find." Chris approached the trash bin. The dog scurried to the edge of the woods still watching for handouts. Chris dumped the garbage bags inside the container and headed for the back door. "Don't go anywhere. I'll be right back."

The canine tilted his head and barked.

"Okay, I'll hurry." Chris headed into the kitchen where Doug flipped burgers. "Can you make me an extra?"

The cook eyed him with interest but tossed another hamburger onto the grill. "Is this for that mangy mut that's been hanging around?" He raised his eyebrows.

Chris didn't respond. So, what if he had a soft spot for animals? Big deal.

"Whatever you say, boss." Doug pulled a basket of fries out of hot grease.

Chris pushed through the kitchen door and entered the dining room. He had owned Dog-Tired Bar and Grill for five years now. He had worked there as a teenager, and when old man Joe retired and announced the grill was either closing or for sale, Chris scraped together every penny he'd saved over the years by doing odds and ends jobs. He'd also tapped into a trust fund that his estranged grandmother had willed to him, a trust he hadn't been allowed to touch until he turned twenty-five. Chris had never withdrawn a cent until the restaurant became available. Locals thought he was too young to own the restaurant, but he did nothing the ordinary way. His abnormal childhood had taught him that he was different than other people, good or bad.

Kat, a dining room attendant right out of high school, stood on a stool, stringing the blasted awful Christmas lights across the top of the doorway. Chris despised Christmas, always had, and he planned to do the bare minimum as usual for the holiday, which was why Kat hung the lights instead of him. Otherwise, he'd have no decorations at all. He had never liked the holiday, and his fiancée breaking up with him the prior Christmas Eve hadn't helped.

"Don't you think it's too early to hang those?" He knew his voice sounded grouchy but didn't change his tone. "It's not even Thanksgiving yet."

"The earlier the better." Kat continued to hang the lights.

Except for the three women catching up with each other, the restaurant wasn't busy at two o'clock. The women were the town's gossips. Every small town had them—Mindy, Mandy, and Melissa. The Three M's. Chris didn't know why, but he found the similarity of their names amusing.

Doug brought their order to the table since the servers didn't clock in until four thirty. One good aspect of holidays was this storybook mountain town always attracted tourists and increased business.

"Your mutt's hamburger is ready," Doug said on his way back to the kitchen.

As much as Chris would love to own a dog, he worked too many hours, and his old house and hardwood floors were drafty and uninviting for pets. He'd settle for feeding the dog whenever the animal stopped by for a visit. The dog likely frequented several restaurants along Main Street, such as the Mountain Diner, Grandma's Kitchen, and a fancy steak restaurant called Beefs.

Chris returned to the kitchen and snatched the to-go box holding the breadless burger. "Thanks." He took the container outside, but the dog wasn't there. He whistled but still nothing. He set the box on the ground, hoping it didn't attract a wild animal.

His cell phone rang, and Ashley's name popped up. "Hey there. What's up?" She was either calling for help or wanting to bug him about the Candlelight Tour.

"I'm looking over the event I inherited and what a mess. The woman who quit barely started organizing anything, and we only have six weeks left."

Here it was. The event committee asked him every year.

"Sorry to hear about your situation, but the answer is no."

Silence ensued. "I haven't asked you anything yet. But now that you mentioned it, will you list your house in the Candlelight Home Tour?"

"No. I have no interest in loading Amelia House with Christmas decorations just to take them back down again in a few weeks. Not only is that a lot of work, but my home is in desperate need of a makeover."

"What if I find someone to help you decorate?"

"Nope."

She sighed into the phone. "My cousin might come to town. I can't wait for you to meet her, and she might agree to help you."

Chris counted to three before he responded. "Stop right there. Do not play matchmaker in my life, and don't add my house to your list for the Candlelight Tour. I detest Christmas, and my home is my personal space despite what little time I spend there."

Ashley giggled into the phone as though she didn't take his answer seriously. "We'll see about that."

By the time he got home to relax on the couch for the night, it was ten o'clock. He popped open a bottle of Brown Bear, a dark ale from a local brewery and a popular choice at Dog-Tired Bar and Grill.

He glanced around his living room, imagining it outfitted for Christmas. If he were being honest, it was obvious a governor no longer owned Amelia House as a personal mountain retreat. He scrutinized the faded hardwood floors, the scratched antique coffee table in front of him, and the neglected oak railing of the grand staircase leading upstairs. It would take a team to prepare his house for a Candlelight Tour. But the undertaking might be beneficial if Ashley's cousin agreed to renovate his home in exchange for participating in the event.

Chris pegged Brittany as a bubbly woman, full of life, intellectual, but more reserved than Ashley. It seemed impossible to feel attracted to her by video chat, but he did. Curiosity was trying to grab hold of him, but he wasn't ready to date again.

The breakup last year hurt too much. He was no longer heartbroken but wary of trusting anyone again.

He forced his thoughts away from Brittany and back to decorating for an event that lasted a ridiculous, meager couple of hours. Never once had he adorned these rooms for any holiday. One could argue that he barely decorated his home enough to live there daily. It lacked the cozy touch he wished it possessed but had no idea how to achieve. There were a few leftover nuances from his ex-fiancée, such as the fine-laced curtains that feminized the living room. She also left behind two chunky white candles on his mantel that added a sense of hominess. Unfortunately, the fireplace had been converted to gas due to the age of the house and chimney. He preferred the smell of real wood burning, but a small firepit out back on the deck solved that problem.

The silence of his home drove him crazy tonight. Normally, he loved the peaceful break from the noise of the restaurant, but not this evening. Sometimes loneliness grabbed hold of him and refused to let go. Another reason to avoid the holidays so he didn't feel that pain. He had no family to help mute the bad memories.

Chris clicked on the TV mounted above the fireplace, but romantic Christmas movies flooded his choices. Did people really watch this stuff? Romance like that didn't exist.

CHAPTER TWO

The drive took longer than expected. Once I reached the mountains, I misjudged the distance to Snow Valley. The stops I'd made to take photos at several breathtaking overlooks hadn't helped.

The fiery sun began to dip low in the sky, skimming the surface of the rolling purple mountains. The wide spans of sky revealed neon yellow, orange, and peach, but it was the wide layer of cerulean blue, topped off with a long strip of wavy dark clouds, that caught my attention.

Stunning was too small of a word to describe the beauty. I had forgotten how much I loved the mountains.

The loud sound of crunching gravel made me gasp. I swerved back onto the road, my heart beating fast as I scolded myself for glancing at the sky. Edging the winding road ahead, I tried to pay close attention to the curves, but I found it impossible not to notice the bare limbs mixed among dark shades of thick Fraser fir trees. A smattering of shadowed houses peeked out from the forest. I hit the button to roll down the window. The smell of winter and wood burning fireplaces filled the car, and I grinned as I inhaled the refreshing mountain scent.

I had wanted to reach Ashley's house before night to avoid the dark curves leading to town, but no such luck. Inky blackness settled in and engulfed the landscape at a fast pace. I drew in a long breath and tried to relax my tight grip on the steering wheel as I slowed around a sharp, hairpin turn. I tried not to imagine the steep drop off on the righthand side that loomed like a stalker in the night. At least it wasn't snowing or raining, and the pavement was dry.

After what seemed to take forever, the twinkling lights of the town came into view. As I drove through the quiet streets, only a handful of open restaurants welcomed me. Hungry and unable to wait any longer, I wanted to stop for a quick bite to eat.

A brick building with a large window overlooking the street snagged my attention. A hand-painted logo of a dog on a sign announced Dog-Tired Bar and Grill. I related well to feeling dog-tired, so I parked out front, two spots down from the entrance. Grabbing my purse off the passenger seat, I climbed from my Camry and stretched, the cold mountain air seeping into my bones. I had forgotten how chilly the North Carolina mountains could be in winter. But wow! I loved how the strong scent of Fraser firs made the town smell like Christmas.

I reached in to grab my lightweight coat off the passenger seat. I'd need to buy a thicker one if I stayed up here for any length of time.

The heavy door of Dog-Tired surprised me, and as I opened it, the wind took hold and blew the door into me. The sheer weight about knocked me over. Once safely inside, the pleasant ambience surprised me, and Christmas lights made the place feel cheery. A younger woman greeted me with a smile and showed me to a wooden booth across from the bar where a few men watched the overhead game in silence. The bartender stood nearby, hanging out with the gentlemen.

I did a doubletake. The bartender looked familiar and about my age, handsome in a slightly rugged way with a neat and tidy chocolate-brown beard, short hair, a blue flannel shirt, and a set of biceps the long sleeves refused to hide. His muscles begged for attention from a woman's hands.

But not my hands!

I was up here to help my cousin and get back home as soon as possible. Besides, I lived at the coast, and he lived here. No thanks. I never wanted to entertain a long-distance relationship again.

He glanced up, catching me staring at him. Turning my attention away, I plucked the menu from the table that the server left behind. A photo of a juicy hamburger and golden fries invited me to order the platter, along with a tall glass of ice water and a pale ale, some local brand with a brown bear on its label.

I felt him studying me. I swear he resembled Ashley's friend, but I wasn't a hundred percent sure. We had poor lighting when we had talked on video chat. When I glanced up, he turned his gaze away.

After ordering, I beelined toward the bathroom. When I finished, I opened the door and practically bumped into the handsome guy, catching a brief whiff of his woodsy cologne. I missed the scent of a man, of having his arms wrapped around me in a warm embrace. It had been at least two years since I had dated, mostly due to my devotion to running Time-Worn Treasures.

"Excuse me, ma'am." He reached out to shake my hand with Southern politeness and a soft mountain drawl. "I'm Chris Hart."

Chris Hart. I was right! My cheeks burned warm, an annoying tell-tale blush I had dealt with all my life when it came to talking to the opposite sex. "I'm Brittany Adams. Pleased to meet you."

His eyebrows raised as if he recognized me. "Adams … as in related to Ashley Adams? Are you the woman I talked to on video chat?" he asked with a hint of curiosity in his voice.

"Yes, that's me."

"Ashley is a friend of mine, and I believe you and I talked on the phone."

He was every bit of what I imagined and had to wonder if Ashley was dating him. Lucky girl!

He glanced toward the doorway as if he needed to get back to work but then turned back to me. "First time in town?"

"Actually, my second, but I haven't been here in a few years. It was a short trip back then, but I'm here for a while this time."

"Welcome back. Let me know if you need anything and enjoy your meal. It's on the house."

"Thank you," I called to his back as he made a quick exit from the hallway. Amazing how I had been in town less than a few minutes and had already met the man I'd been curious about. T'was the Christmas season and all its glorious magic.

I nibbled on the last bite of hamburger as I decided to pay my own bill. I didn't see Chris anywhere … not that I necessarily wanted to talk to him again anyway since he was likely dating Ashley. The drive to Ashley's house was a short drive, and when I pulled into the driveway, a flood light clicked on to break the monotonous dark.

I opened the back of my Toyota and unloaded two large suitcases. They were heavy as always, no matter the length of my trip, and I huffed when pulling them out of the trunk. My mom had questioned why I packed so much, but for once I had a valid excuse. Tonight marked the first day of my six-week stint in the mountains unless I could leave earlier. A quick trip. Winter clothes demanded a lot more suitcase space than packing summer dresses for a Caribbean destination, my ideal setting. Warm weather and humidity, as well as bright blue water, spoke to my heart. I never wanted to live somewhere cold and snowy.

Just the thought made me shiver in my flimsy jacket as I rolled my suitcases toward the walkway. A row of solar lights lit the large, carefully placed flat stones leading to the front door. The air smelled crisp, instead of like salty beach. For a moment, a hint of nostalgia crept in about not spending family time together for Thanksgiving or Christmas with my parents, but the choice hadn't been mine to make.

The steep climb made me huff, and my suitcases' wheels weren't made for the gaps between the rugged stones. When a wheel got stuck, I tugged hard, almost toppling over when the crack released its hold. Next time I'd make two trips.

Oversized holly bushes shouldered one side of the walkway, and the solar lamps lined the other. Ashley had mentioned fixing up the house, but from what I could tell in the dark, she had also done a fantastic job with the landscaping.

When I reached the top of the stairs and stood in front of the mountain cottage, a note taped to the door fluttered in the wind. *Come In, Brittany.*

I knocked briefly to announce my arrival and pushed open the door. The smell of cinnamon greeted me, reminding me of Nana's home. Ashley and I used to love visiting on Saturday afternoons as kids. She always had a cup of hot cocoa, a plate of freshly baked cookies, and a deck of cards on the table. We stayed for hours, chatting up Nana and telling her about school, boys, friends, and asking for advice.

A tinge of longing ached in my chest.

"Ashley?" I called out through the empty hallway. The kitchen was dark, as was a formal dining room made into an office, but soft Christmas music played from a doorway down the hall. Though Ashley and I shared a passion for Christmas, she usually got into the holiday spirit a couple weeks before me.

"In here on the couch," Ashley called out.

I approached the doorway and did a double take at the sight of her lying flat on the couch. She wasn't one to stay still long. Her unkempt strawberry blonde hair surprised me too, usually brushed and shiny or braided. A familiar blue-and-white quilt that Nana had made covered her all the way to her neck. Living in the Great Smokey Mountains had been Ashley's childhood dream after attending yearly summer camps near Snow Valley, and here she was, living up here without family nearby.

I entered the dimly lit room. Colored lights blinked on a small Christmas tree and a holiday movie played on the television. "Hey, Cuz. It's great to see you again," I said, leaning down to hug her with care.

"You too, but I wish it were under different circumstances." Ashley wore her right arm in a sling and had a collection of water bottles and medication sprawled across the nearby coffee table. She winced as she bent her knees up to make room for me to sit by her. "I'm so glad you are here, but I was starting to get worried. I thought you'd arrive a couple of hours ago." She grimaced when she moved.

"Sorry about that. I tried to call earlier but didn't have service in the mountains." I sat gently at the edge of the couch. "I should have called when I stopped for dinner at Dog-Tired Bar and Grill." Ashley always treated me like a little sister, and I loved and missed her. I always wanted siblings, especially a sister, and loving Ashley filled my heart.

Her face lit up. "Did you meet Chris?"

I tried to fight a smile but my face turned warm. "Yes, I did. Tell me more about the two of you."

She grinned too big, making me believe she did have feelings for him.

"He's the sweetest man ever, although he's always working and he's closed off emotionally. He had a bad breakup with his fiancée. Turns out she dumped him for an ex-boyfriend, apparently never letting go of the dream of being with her high school sweetheart." Ashley paused to catch her breath after talking so fast, a habit of hers. Everyone always loved her outgoing and charismatic personality. She inhaled a long breath to begin her next stretch of explanation. "She went back to her hometown for a class reunion, leaving Chris behind, and when she returned, she broke the engagement off. It was pitiful to see him mope around for months. Guess you could say he still does to some extent, and it's been a year."

A little tug pulled at my heart for Chris, having been discarded before his wedding. Poor guy.

Ashley's attention diverted to a pile of paperwork and an overstuffed box on the table. I caught a glimpse of a notebook and a thick binder poking from the opened lid. "Is that for work?"

Ashley frowned and winced when she tried to pull the binder from the box. I grabbed the carton and set it on the floor next to her.

"Yes, the woman who quit left these on her desk. Since our small company specializes in events, without currently having an event planner, the job fell into my lap. And now I can barely get off the couch or adjust my clothing in the bathroom. How am I going to plan a Candlelight Tour?"

My guard went up now after seeing the stuffed box and files, though I knew I'd help her with whatever she needed. That was what family did.

"Can't you take vacation pay?"

"Sure, but someone has to do the job, so it'll be waiting for me when I return to work. The event will come fast."

"I'm here for you," I said in response, fighting off a groan. Ashley's eyebrows drew in a straight line, but knowing what she was about to say, I stopped her. "And no, I won't take your pay. You have bills, and I'm still earning a salary from the antique shop."

She frowned but nodded. "I'm not sure if fifteen people could pull off this event, much less the two of us. And I don't have enough homes entered in the tour."

"Shouldn't that be easy to fix? I'd think everyone would love the honor."

Ashley shook her head. "Not even close. Decorating their home and offering appetizers can be a lot of work. We do offer prizes, as well as fifty-dollar gift cards for Dog-Tired Bar and Grill just for participating, and a handful of other donations from sponsors."

"Sounds tempting to me. If you give me a list of names and addresses for homes you'd like on the tour, I can introduce myself as your cousin and ask them to join. Would that help?"

"It couldn't hurt and thank you." Ashley tried to reach for her bottle of water but screeched.

Feeling sorry for her, I passed the bottle to her, wondering how she planned to use the restroom after drinking so much fluid. I reached out for the binder marked Candlelight Home Tour and flicked on the lamp near me. I paged through the photos. "Gorgeous homes! Are they all downtown?"

"Yes, within walking distance of each other." She gulped more water then handed the bottle to me to place on the coffee table. "The house I want most on the tour is Chris's home, but he refuses."

"Why won't he list his home? And please tell me you're dating him." I was being presumptuous, but I wanted to know the situation.

Ashley laughed, winced, then smiled all dreamy-like. "I wish, but we aren't dating. We're more like family. I had a crush on him once, but he wasn't interested."

Yikes. "Sounds disappointing."

"Nah, not anymore. Besides, I have him earmarked for you." Her words didn't quite match her tone, and I suspected she still had hidden feelings for him, even if she refused to admit the truth to herself.

I shook my head with determination. "I don't need a set-up." True, he was handsome, sweet as pie, and a business owner, all great qualities in a man, but if Ashley held the slightest attraction toward Chris, then it was best to leave the thought alone.

Unfortunately, my heart rate picked up just thinking about him. "Why won't he join the Candlelight Tour?"

Ashley shrugged and rolled her eyes. "He works all the time and says his house isn't ready for people to parade through. And he's right, his home isn't ready."

"All acceptable reasons. What if we help him?"

Ashley flicked her chin toward her arm. "I do need surgery in two days. Fixing up his house isn't going to happen soon enough unless you're willing to help. That'd be a big favor to ask."

I stilled, trying not to react so she didn't suspect my attraction toward him. The next six weeks were going to prove difficult if I couldn't avoid him. But the problem was, I hadn't met anyone else quite like him.

Ashley tilted her head toward me. "Promise you'll do whatever's necessary to convince Chris to enter his house in the Candlelight Tour?"

CHAPTER THREE

Chris knelt outside on the back patio behind Dog-Tired, holding an open to-go box in his outstretched hand. "Bite-sized pieces of slow-cooked roast beef. It's good stuff."

The black dog tilted his head and whined. He stretched his neck forward and sniffed the air.

"Go on. I'm safe." Chris set the box on the ground.

More sniffs, then with hesitance the dog stepped forward, sniffed again, and gently took a piece of meat from the container. The sample must have passed his approval because he dove in and gobbled the roast beef as if he hadn't eaten in days.

"That's right. Good boy." Chris held out his hand with hope the dog would close the distance between them, but no chance. After finishing the meal, he slinked a couple of feet away. No worries because Chris understood all too well how it took time to trust people. "If we keep meeting like this, I'll have to give you a name."

The dog tilted his head as if trying to decipher Chris's words.

"We can hang lost-and-found signs up in town, but in the meantime, you need a name. Let's see." Chris scratched his temple to think. "Brown." The dog whined in answer, so Chris scratched his temple again. "Scruff? Bone? Wait! How about Bo?"

The dog gave a short bark.

"Great, Bo it is." Chris reached out, and while the dog seemed timid as if maybe someone had hit him before, he allowed Chris to touch his scruff. "Good boy. I don't know your past, but I can guarantee your future will look much better if you stick around." Chris aimed his phone at Bo and snapped several flattering photos.

Doug opened the back door and poked his head through the opening. "Just thought you might want to know that your dream girl is here to order lunch."

Chris glanced up, raising his eyebrows. "My dream girl? I didn't realize I have one."

"I saw the way you looked at Ashley's cousin last night. Anyway, thought you'd like to know."

After Doug ducked back inside, Chris timed out three minutes on his watch, so he didn't seem eager to head back to the dining room to see Brittany. Once he entered, he made a pit stop in the restroom to doublecheck his appearance since he owned the place.

He walked out of the restroom and into the dining room, noticing her immediately. She sat at a corner table by a window with the view of the light snow falling. She wrapped her hands around a mug of hot chocolate with whipped cream on top. As he headed toward the bar, she glanced up. He changed his direction and walked over to her to be friendly.

"Good morning," she said with a soft smile.

He greeted her in return. If he didn't know better, she seemed almost happy to see him. Had he spent so much time in his head about his breakup with Dana that he hadn't noticed other women taking interest in him? While his emotions wanted to protect him from another hurtful relationship, logic reminded him he was lonely and needed to risk his heart again.

Brittany motioned for him to join her at the table. He was working, but what the heck. He pulled out the chair and sat across from her, nodding toward Kat to bring him a cup of his usual black coffee.

"How's Snow Valley treating you so far?" he asked. He shifted in his seat, not normally feeling unsettled by attractive customers.

"I haven't seen much, but Ashley is the best." She sipped from her mug, not taking her eyes off him.

He mentally shrugged off her gaze, trying not to overthink the curious expression on her face. "I could show you around since Ashley isn't able to play tour guide at the moment."

Why had he offered? He was working.

Her features brightened with surprise. "I'd love that, if you aren't too busy." She glanced around his empty restaurant. It was a little early for the lunch rush.

"How about two-thirty?" That gave him plenty of time to help during lunch and he could be back before the dinner began. "Anything in particular you want to see?"

"Downtown, the mountains in the daylight, and maybe the homes on the Candlelight Home Tour."

He cringed. "I've got you covered for downtown and the mountains."

"But not the Candlelight Tour?" She looked puzzled.

He cleared his throat. "Christmas isn't my thing."

She leaned forward as if wanting to question him about the certainty in his tone, but then she sat back in the chair. Chris wasn't ready to explain why he despised Christmas. It wasn't anyone's business. Dana was the only one who knew his past, and since moving to Snow Valley after college, where he had met Ashley, he didn't feel the need to share his history.

"Ashley says you have a beautiful historic home. I own an antique shop at the beach, so I'm fascinated by history." Her face lit up with interest. "I'd love to know how old it is."

"1849. My home is called Amelia House and is Greek Revival style, with a massive two-story portico in front that new owners added in the early 20th century."

Her eyes widened. Curiosity maybe?

"I'm sorry you don't enjoy Christmas, but your house sounds amazing. Have you considered joining the Candlelight Tour?"

He shook his head again, adamant. "Like I said, Christmas isn't my thing. With running this restaurant, I don't have time to decorate, much less to renovate it for a public tour."

"I can relate to lack of time, but if the house is in disrepair, that makes signing up for an event even more daunting of a task. Business comes first like a child."

"Exactly. Most people don't understand." He stared at her. As a shop owner, she obviously comprehended the number of hours he poured into the restaurant to make it profitable. She made him feel heard.

Brittany stared at him with startling blue eyes, the shade of the deep Atlantic Ocean. He'd attended a business conference once in Daytona, and he could stare endlessly into her eyes just as he had with the sea from his ocean-front balcony.

She tapped the table, averting his gaze. "If it's not an imposition, I'd love to see Amelia House sometime. Historic homes are a connection to the past. The way people lived back then is fascinating to me, as well as the intricate woodwork and architecture of the houses."

"We can add that to your tour today." He grinned when she sat up straighter in her chair. "Anything else you want to see?" He had surprised himself by agreeing to let her come inside his home. No one ever came over. They had tried, but the sacred space was his alone. She seemed more interested in the history of the house than trying to work her way into his life, though. After his breakup, he wasn't interested in dating.

"Well, I'd like to check out some of the charming shops, such as Aunt Sally's Boutique, Daisy's Gift Shoppe, and Mountain Candles. Mountain Wood Carvings sounds interesting too, and maybe the Squirrel Nut and Snow Valley Pottery."

"All great choices."

They agreed to meet later and parted ways while she finished eating. Midafternoon she showed up at Dog-Tired smelling fresh like cinnamon, which he recognized as the scent from Ashley's house. Brittany's hair, a rich brown hue, reminded him of the inside of M&Ms®, except her auburn highlights resembled autumn itself. She wore an orange and burnt umber flannel jacket that he knew belonged to Ashley.

"Is that the heaviest coat you have?" he asked, leaning against the bar. She'd never make it in the freezing mountain temperatures.

"I didn't realize how cold it is up here." Her cheeks were pink, and she crossed her arms as if she were already chilly.

"If you're here for the next six weeks, you'll need something warmer than what you are wearing. We will have snow. I have an extra ski jacket you can borrow, but we should stop and buy you gloves, a hat, and a scarf."

She stared at him, her mouth dropping open. "Snow? I realize there are snow flurries now, but a full-fledged snowfall?"

He chuckled, finding Brittany's naivety of weather in a mountain town during the winter season adorable. "Guaranteed."

"We haven't gotten snow at the beach in eight years, and, even then, it only lasted for an hour before it melted. Thanks for the offer of the ski jacket. I saw an outdoor shop at the edge of town as I drove in last night. Maybe they'll have accessories."

"Any clothing shop here will offer those items, but if you want a hand-knit scarf and hat, I suggest Aunt Sally's Boutique. I have ski gloves you can borrow."

"Very thoughtful of you."

Chris nodded. "I'm ready to go if you are. I thought we'd stop by my house first to pick up those items, and I can show you Amelia House. Then we can drive around town so I can show you the homes on the tour. Are you be helping Ashley plan?"

She nodded but didn't press him on including his house on the Candlelight Tour.

As they drove, light snowfall continued to come down, and he turned on the wipers of his red F-250 truck. When they pulled into his driveway, she gasped, her face glowing with excitement. "Stunning!"

Viewing his brick two-story house from her perspective gave him renewed gratitude. He stopped without turning the truck off so she could take it all in.

"I love the white columns and long porch. And the red clay tiles for the roof!" She pointed to a gas lamp out front. "Does it work?"

"Absolutely. Everything is operational in my home, but it does still need a makeover."

"I bet the gardens are gorgeous in the spring." She was referring to the dormant mountain laurels, rhododendrons, and azaleas in a short, walled-off garden in his front yard.

"Thanks. I can't take credit for maintaining the gardens. I hire a professional service to maintain the yard and gardens to preserve the original appearance of Amelia House." She appreciated his home in ways he hadn't in years.

She pointed to a grouping of large Fraser firs growing in the side yard. "I buy a fresh tree every year for Christmas," she said in awe. "And the magnolia trees!" He had several planted here and there throughout his large yard.

"Yes, the blooms in the gardens are beautiful." He didn't confess that he never put up a Christmas tree.

The garden and features of the old house had captivated him from the beginning, and while he bought the home before it began to deteriorate, with what little free time he had, the maintenance kept him busy. When the upkeep became too much, he had to hire help.

Chris drove along the far side of the home, passing the old well house and servants' quarters, and parked the truck in front of the garage.

"Was your garage once a carriage house?" She took in the four-car garage, and he was almost embarrassed by her overzealous appreciation of his home.

"Yes, you're observant."

He resisted the urge to hold her hand as he led her along the sidewalk to the front to give her the full experience of history by walking through the front door.

She beamed as they stepped into the long foyer, which consisted of several doorways, a narrow rug running almost the full length that ended with a grandfather clock. A wooden staircase on the right side led to a landing with another freestanding clock.

"I can't believe you live here. Lucky you!" She ran her hand along the slick surface of the banister he'd managed to polish this past week.

"Thank you." Chris's cheeks grew warm at her grandiose compliments as he removed his coat and folded it across the back of an antique chair that she was now admiring. "The house still needs a lot of work, but I lack the available attention it deserves."

His embarrassment grew as he took a slower look around his place.

The hardwood floors practically screamed at him for a good polishing. In addition, the living room walls needed a paint job. The upstairs required both painting and floor polish, as well as a talented interior designer.

"Just cosmetic things, nothing too big," she said, glancing into each room on the lower floor, respecting the closed door of his bedroom.

"You're optimistic."

She shook her head. "This is a beautiful home. It would be a blessing to everyone if you put it in the Candlelight Home Tour."

There it was. He was so tired of everyone pushing him to enter his house. He stiffened, not knowing what to say.

Brittany placed her hand gently on his elbow. "I'm sorry. I got excited and shouldn't have crossed that boundary. You said no to the Candlelight Tour, and I respect your decision."

His guard lowered. She was different than the other women in town. She didn't appear to have an agenda, but instead awe filled her and admiration for the history Amelia House represented. What a relief.

He pulled open the hall closet and retrieved his favorite ski jacket and a pair of gloves.

"This should keep you warm enough." He handed the worn items to her, but she was busy eyeing the few antiques he owned. "Snow Valley will get colder than you think, and you have to prepare. I'd also keep a blanket in your car."

She tilted her head. "A blanket?"

"In case your vehicle gets stuck in the snow on the side of the road. A backpack will help too. Fill it with snacks, a flashlight, and an additional layer of clothes. Bring water with you when you leave the house." He had to smile at the astonished gaze in her eyes. "I have an extra snow shovel and a bag of salt you can put in the back."

She shook her head quickly, as if overwhelmed. "I'm sorry, but will I need all those supplies? Can't I just call for a tow truck?"

He laughed, the low rumble filling the space between them. "Sure, if they can get to you. It's a busy time of year for them." He pointed to the jacket and gloves. "This way you'll be prepared. And always keep your cell phone charged, although service is spotty out here. A waterproof phone case is a good purchase."

"I'm positive that I'm not cut out for mountain living." She grimaced, and they both started laughing. "Ashley failed to tell me all the drawbacks before I drove up here."

"You'll do fine. Just call if you need me." He had no idea why he kept offering himself to her, but she was out of her element in a new town, knowing no one except for her cousin. "How's Ashley doing?"

Brittany glanced up.

Feeling as though he had to explain his friendship with Ashley, he said, "We go back to college years. She's a good friend."

Brittany nodded, but he got the feeling she didn't quite believe him. He'd always known Ashley crushed on him, but he thought of her as the sister he didn't have, despite townsfolk who tried to fix them up constantly. He didn't have time to date. A business owner could never grow complacent, especially during the winter season.

Popular ski slopes drove tourists into town, as well as the quaint holiday cheer of small-town Snow Valley. The hype was overrated in his opinion, but he wasn't one to turn away business just because he didn't share their sentiment.

He gave Brittany a quick tour of the rest of the house, pleased by the excitement on her face.

"The kitchen is amazing and is a chef's dream!" Her enthusiasm made her look like a child opening a present to find her favorite surprise gift staring back at her.

"Do you enjoy cooking?" He did, hence the state-of-the-art kitchen appliances.

She glanced around at the granite counter tops and stainless steel. "I've always wanted to learn but never did. Guess I'm too busy with running my store. I usually buy fast food whenever possible or buy dinner at one of three of my favorite restaurants. Let's just say learning to cook, or maybe bake, is on my bucket list."

"I can teach you how."

Why did he offer himself again, as though he had endless free time? She was a capable, independent woman, who didn't need to hang out with him. She was here to help Ashley because of her injury. Period.

"That would be wonderful." She placed her hand on his arm, her warmth seeping through his long-sleeved shirt. There was something liberating about her touch that urged him to let go of the past.

He shook off the thought. Their eyes met for a prolonged moment.

"Ready to see the town?" he asked, placing a hand on her back to steer her toward the front door.

"Of course." Her cheeks reddened, but she led the way through the hallway. She paused to glance into the living room once more. "With a few Christmas decorations, I can almost imagine this house in the past with its holiday parties. I can see a butler offering drinks to guests, staff walking around with trays of hors d'oeuvres, and people dressed in formal clothes. What a beautiful image."

Interesting because he'd had his own visions of past parties and family in this house, as if the home begged for people to enjoy its beauty once more.

CHAPTER FOUR

I stared out the passenger side of the truck's window at delicate, falling flakes. A thin layer of white covered the branches of evergreens in people's yards, making the town look more like Christmas, even though it was only November. The houses signed up for the Candlelight Tour resembled mansions but didn't come close to touching the beauty of Amelia House.

I didn't mind the cold outside as long as the heater in Chris's truck continued to blow out a steady stream of heat to warm my chilled fingers and toes. Even though he had loaned me a ski jacket and much-appreciated gloves, we still stopped to purchase a handcrafted knit hat and matching scarf from the quaint store he recommended. All I had left to buy was a pair of boots.

Now, as we drove down a narrow street, he pointed to a large white house at the edge of town. "This is a favorite on the Candlelight Tour. An older couple owns the home. The husband is a retired doctor from Asheville."

I marveled at the towering house, likely dating back to the 1800s. "I can see why it's a favorite, although your house has it beat. Not that it's a competition."

His glanced over at me. "You're quite generous, although I think you have a bias for Amelia House. She's easy to love."

"True statement. Your house would definitely be the new favorite if it were on the tour." As soon as I said the words, he stiffened. "Sorry, but I can't help wishing you'd share her beauty with the public. She's a prize."

I let the topic drop, but I meant what I said.

We drove through the streets of Snow Valley. He showed me houses that were competing for the Historical Preservation Award, as well as the Community Spirit Award. I knew without a doubt that Amelia House would win either of these prizes if Chris made a commitment.

"I hope you reconsider."

He studied me but didn't press the subject.

I promised I'd help Ashley with the Candlelight Tour, but I had a hunch that if he didn't agree to join the tour, Ashley would likely lose her job.

His hold on the steering wheel tightened. "Are you going to join the others in pushing this event on me too?"

"What if I told you Ashley needed your help?"

He clenched his jaw and grimaced.

I'd let the subject go for now, but I wasn't finished with the topic yet.

We drove by a long brick house that someone had converted into a commercial property, but it now appeared abandoned. "What's the story about this house? I'm intrigued." The structure had good bones, as my dad had liked to say as a real estate broker.

Chris turned into the large parking lot to appease my interest in the building. "It was a failing carpet store. Let's check it out."

He didn't have to say it twice. As soon as he parked out front, I climbed out of the truck. The wind had picked up and howled, but the worsening weather didn't keep me from checking out the cool building. I reached and pulled on the large brass handle of the door, but it was locked. "Bummer. I was hoping on the off chance it was open."

"No such luck. Half of the wood is missing on the far window." He headed toward the corner of the house, and I hurried behind him to catch up. It looked as if someone had pried part of the plywood off to see inside. Apparently, I wasn't the only one curious about the building.

I stepped close to Chris, cupping my hands against the glass to peer inside. Goosebumps ran down my spine, and I wasn't sure if it was the abandoned building, or if it was because I stood so close to Chris that our arms touched. Even through our coats I felt his warmth.

Choosing to ignore my attraction to him, I said, "Wow, look at this place." Several rolls of carpet had been left behind on a dirty wooden floor. Even though the place was messy, I recognized how beautiful it could be. The inside of the store still resembled a home where someone had once lived. The old fireplace and mantel reminded me of Amelia House.

"Wish we could see more." Apparently, the home intrigued Chris as well.

I stepped back. "I wonder what's upstairs."

"If I recall correctly, the owners had made it into an apartment and lived up there." A wind gust kicked up, and Chris shoved his bare hands into the pockets of his coat. Thankfully, the gloves and coat he loaned me kept me warm. "When their store failed," he continued to say, "they moved back to the city but left the house in disrepair. I'm not sure if it was foreclosed on, or if they just left it behind for their family to someday inherit."

"How someone could leave this behind makes no sense to me." We headed back to the truck and drove to Dog-Tired, which was about how I felt. Dog-tired. All the driving yesterday and today got to me, plus the vicious wind now left my face and feet chilled.

The cup of hot chocolate that Chris promised at the end of our tour sounded good. He parked on the street next to my car and a few spots down from the restaurant entrance.

Chris hurried around and opened the door for me. When I stepped from the truck, my feet slipped on ice. His strong arms caught and steadied me from the sheer speed of my near fall. Time seemed to slow as he held me close. A set of unfamiliar butterflies danced through my belly.

"Thank you."

He placed me upright, keeping his hand on my back but wiggling his eyebrows up and down with humor. We were so close I could smell peppermint on his breath.

"As soon as you opened your door, I had the intuition that you were going to slip. It's not as though you are used to walking on ice." Chris stayed close enough in case I slipped again as we headed toward the restaurant. He held open the door, and I caught a glimpse of several patrons sitting at tables and the server that I had met on the first day of my arrival to town hustling around.

Chris ignored their stares but the sudden interest in us made me uncomfortable. He chose a booth near the front window, so I was able to watch the continued snowfall. Already, a thin layer of snow started accumulating on the sideview mirrors of his truck, but it melted on the hood as soon as it landed due to the warmth of the engine.

When the server approached, Chris made the introductions. "Kat, this is Brittany. She's Ashley's cousin and is here to help since she broke her shoulder."

"So nice to meet you," Kat said, shaking my hand. "We've met before, but not formally. Welcome to our town, and I hope you're finding your way around." She studied me, as if realizing Chris and I had spent the afternoon together. "Aren't you going to be helping Ashley with the Candlelight Tour?"

Out of the corner of my eye, I noticed Chris straighten, muscles tensed.

"She's asked me to help her, but I don't know the first thing about planning events. I just want to make her life a bit easier."

Chris leaned against the back of the wooden bench, appearing to relax a bit more but not completely.

"That is nice of you," Kat said, smiling at me. She seemed friendly. "Ashley mentioned you need more houses for the tour. I tried talking my parents into enlisting ours, but they said they had to think about it."

"I'm sure Ashley appreciates your help. Why do you think people are hesitant about joining?"

Kat glanced over at Chris. "Some people think it's too much work for a few hours of the tour, and it's also late notice."

I had guessed as much when Ashley first mentioned the lack of participation. "That makes sense. The woman who oversaw the Candlelight Tour quit suddenly, without having the final details in place. Now Ashley is scrambling to get enough people to make the event worth having. She needs several more participants."

Chris studied me with interest, but I didn't want to put him on the spot in front of Kat, so I refrained from including him in the discussion.

Kat tucked a long, light-brown strand of hair behind her ear. "But the tour is important to the Christmas festivities. I'll talk to my parents again. Maybe the committee needs to offer more of an incentive."

As far as I knew, the committee consisted of Ashley and me. If other people were involved, I wasn't aware. "Thanks, I appreciate your help. We need all we can get."

After Kat walked away, Chris tapped his fork on the table, seemingly lost in thought.

"A penny for your thoughts," I said, curious as to what he was thinking.

He looked me straight in the eyes. "I know what you're doing, and I don't like it."

My body involuntarily jerked, his comment taking me by surprise. "What do you mean?"

"Spending the day with me to get on my good side so I'll join your Candlelight Tour."

I shook my head to ward off his accusation. "I spent the day with you because you invited me, and I enjoyed our time together."

Our gazes remained locked for a moment. I wasn't about to back down and glance away. He blinked. "Sorry. Guess people have asked me so many times over the years that the subject makes me a little edgy."

"Apology accepted, but I'm curious. The event sounds like a lot of fun and a chance to support your community. Why don't you really want to join in the festivities?"

His mouth dropped open. He started to speak, stopped, and grimaced. "It's a long story."

I settled back against my seat, instinctively knowing not to push him but still waiting in case he wanted to discuss the subject further.

We sipped our hot cocoa silently. When he finished his, he sighed. "Not everyone is happy at Christmas time, you know. The holiday cheer makes it difficult for those who've lost someone, who are hurting."

I placed my hand on his. "I'm sorry if you are in pain."

He swallowed hard and glanced up. "A lot of us are. Is your family driving up here to be with you for the holidays?"

It was my turn to swallow hard. "My parents are going on a river cruise in December, and Ashley *is* family." My emotions bubbled up and my words came out softer and more vulnerable than I wanted.

"I'm sorry. That must be hard for you."

"It is." His empathy felt too intimate. The last I wanted was to have an attraction to a man who lived in the mountains five hours and forty-eight minutes away, or three hundred fifty-one point one miles, from my cozy home and business on the beach.

A slight grin slid across his mouth.

Nope, don't look at his lips.

"Aren't you going to ask me?"

"Ask you what?" I played with my fingers underneath the table. "About what you're sad about, or why you're avoiding Christmas festivities?"

He studied me. "Not that." His voice sounded grumpy. I had apparently asked him the wrong questions.

I sat in confused silence.

"Let's just say I have painful childhood memories that I don't wish to share." He frowned and stared into his empty mug. "I usually spend the holidays alone."

Now I felt like a jerk.

"The answer is yes, I'll do it."

Shaking my head with confusion, I leaned in toward him. "Do what? Join us for Thanksgiving and Christmas dinner?"

He laughed loud enough that people turned to watch us, Kat included. "No, I will do the Candlelight Tour."

I stared at him. "What have I missed in this discussion?"

"I said I'll do the Candlelight Tour. Isn't that what you wanted to know?"

"Of course, everyone wants you involved in the Candlelight Tour, but I hadn't planned on revisiting that subject the rest of the day." Though the thought had been weighing on my mind.

He tilted his head. "You weren't going ask me?"

"That's not what today is about. You said no, and I respect your decision, so don't feel pressured to change your mind about the tour. I wanted to hang out with you because you're fun."

He leaned back against the wooden booth and crossed his arms. He looked perplexed.

"I'm not most people."

Uncrossing his arms, he placed his hands on the table. "You can say that again. My gut instinct says you are authentic, and people seem to like you."

"I appreciate your compliment." His big brown eyes reminded me of a gentle wild dog. He gave off vibes of determination, strength, and loyalty. He touched a soft spot in me that wasn't just physical but emotional. I hadn't dated in almost two years because I wanted to focus on growing my business and didn't have the extra time, let alone the emotional bandwidth to invest in a relationship.

I glanced at my watch. "I need to get going. I appreciate your personal tour of the area, and enjoyed spending time with you, but I don't want to leave Ashley too long by herself." Ashley had said she wanted to take a long nap and had encouraged me to familiarize myself with the town, so I could better help with the Candlelight Tour. That was exactly what I had done but now it was time to get back to her.

Chris stepped out of the booth. He gave me a friendly half-hug. "I had fun today, and anytime you have questions or want help with anything, be sure to ask."

We said our goodbyes. I hurried out the door but my shoe hit a slick patch of ice, my foot shooting out from underneath me. No one was there to catch me this time, and I landed with a thud on hard concrete. The breath rushed out of my lungs, and I gasped from the sharp pain in my ribs.

"Brittany, are you okay?" I heard Chris behind me. His footsteps rushed over. Before I could process everything, he scooped me up in his masculine arms.

I wasn't sure if breathing was harder because of my fall or because he was holding me so snugly against his chest.

Our long gazes lingered until he loosened his grip on me. I stepped back, staring at his gentle brown eyes, his sexy beard, and his luscious lips. "Um, thanks for helping me up."

His Adam's apple moved. "You need to buy boots as soon as possible. The weather is going to get worse." He still held me until I backed away, trying to think, trying to understand why my entire body tingled.

"Buy boots," he called out as I picked my way to the curb.

I turned and waved before opening the car door. He stood on the sidewalk watching me and butterflies swirled in my belly. "I'll buy them tomorrow, and thanks for spending your valuable time with me. I enjoyed the tour."

"We'll talk later," he called out right before I shut my door. I nodded and waved while he stood watching me until I backed my car out of the spot.

When I pulled into Ashley's driveway, I took a moment to think about the afternoon spent with him. Too bad he was off limits. He was a great guy, just not for me.

I entered the house and heard the television on in the living room. I followed the sound.

"Hey there," I said to my cousin, who laid on the couch in her usual position. "Can I get you anything?"

"How about an early dinner? I tried to sleep but it was impossible due to the pain. Thankfully, I had snacks on the coffee table and took my pain killers with them." Ashley tried to sit up but screeched and laid back down. "How was driving around the town? Were you able to locate the houses on the tour and meet anyone?"

A hint of guilt gnawed at me. "Chris took me around and showed me the different homes. He was helpful."

She was staring at my coat. "Isn't that his?"

"Yes, he loaned it to me because my clothes weren't warm enough." I removed the coat and caught a hint of his spicy scent, making me think about our hug. "I bought these from Aunt Sally's Boutique." To divert her attention, I pulled off the hat and scarf, holding them up to show off my new purchases.

"Adorable." Ashley smiled, but then her gaze flitted downward, and she frowned. "You have dirt on your jeans. Did you fall?"

"Sure did. It was slick outside of Dog-Tired. Good thing I didn't get hurt or we'd both be incapacitated, and I wouldn't be able to help you." I rubbed the sore spot on my right hip and winced.

She pointed at my sneakers. "Those won't give you a good grip but if you look in the hall closet, I have several pairs of boots you can use. They're a staple around here in winter."

We used to borrow each other's shoes and clothes as kids and well into our teenage years, so I knew they'd fit.

"Thanks." I backtracked to the hall closet to hang up my outerwear and to check out the boots. I held up a pair of pink rain boots, then camel-brown ones with a warm layer of fleece lining, and at last the duck boots. All of them would work well, but then I noticed a hefty pair of hiking boots and made my choice.

After I cooked dinner, we sat at the countertop to eat, laughing together, and it felt like old times.

"Did you get to know Chris better?" she asked, her question interrupting the joyful mood.

I cocked my head to the side, wondering where she was going with the inquiry. "Is that a trick question?" Her serious demeaner confused me, her smile having been replaced with a straight face.

"Guess I want to know if you brought up the idea of adding his house to the Candlelight Tour."

"I focused on building trust, but the topic did come up. At first, he was guarded about the subject, but as I was leaving, he said he'd do the event." I shrugged, questioning his unexpected decision to participate in something he might regret.

Ashley sat upright and let out a high-pitched squeal. "He agreed? We've been asking him for three years and he always says no. You hang out with him for a few hours, and he says yes?"

A wave of guilt stabbed at me. "We didn't discuss the event in detail. In fact, we were just talking, and he said he'd do it. I had no idea what he agreed to at first until he clarified."

"Wait a minute. You didn't ask him, or talk about it, but he just said yes?"

"Exactly."

"What's the next step?"

I shrugged, shaking my head. "Beats me."

"Well, ask him. That's the only way we'll know for sure."

That was the last question I wanted to ask him. The subject was touchy at best.

"Brittany, the survival of the Candlelight Home Tour is at risk, so please ask him."

I wish I could just avoid conflict like usual. I hadn't asked to be stuck between helping save Ashley's job and signing up a man for the Candlelight Tour who just happens to despise Christmas.

CHAPTER FIVE

The temperature in the valley dropped as a cold front moved in. Bo needed a warm place to sleep.

With the contents of the doghouse spread out in front of him on the patio behind his restaurant, Chris began to organize parts. Bo sprawled out on a dry patch underneath the overhang and watched as Chris scratched his temple. How could a doghouse be so difficult to assemble? He studied the manual with such intensity that Brittany startled him when she walked around the brick wall, the dirt path already covered with an inch of snow.

"Hey there," he said as she joined him. "I see you're wearing appropriate boots now." He didn't want to admit that he was happy to see her again and had been thinking about her for the past couple of days.

She laughed. "How embarrassing." She lifted her foot to show them off. "Ashley's. She had an array of footwear to choose from, so I chose the sturdiest option along with borrowing a pair of wool socks."

"Great decision. You have to keep your tootsies warm around here." He leaned forward and dusted snow off a section of bench, so she had a place to sit. Not one to be left out, Bo got up and demanded pets from her, burying his head in her lap when she sat. "I bet your boyfriend doesn't like you running off at Christmastime."

A shocked expression crossed her face. "Ashley sent me over here to see when we can discuss the Candlelight Tour in more detail." She chewed her lower lip and added, "And no boyfriend. I don't believe in dating."

He tried not to smile. "That's quite a statement, but I get what you mean about not wanting to date. Women hurt the heart."

"Ashley told me about your fiancée. I'm sorry that happened to you."

He glanced down at Bo instead of looking at Brittany. "Ex-fiancée but thanks." He turned his attention back to her. "The Candlelight Tour… Ashley is wasting no time locking me in." He pinched his lips together to keep from expressing his regret about taking on a huge project during the holiday season. Business always picked up this time of year. What had he been thinking?

It might relieve some pressure to know the details involved. He tossed the instruction pamphlet next to a plank of wood to give her his full attention.

"Let's schedule a time to discuss it. When do you have a day off?" Her voice held excitement, making him feel guilty about his lack of enthusiasm.

"A day off?" He chuckled. "I own a restaurant. I never have time off unless I plan it." He rubbed his beard to think. "How about tonight? Let's say eight o'clock at my house. I'll bring a pepperoni pizza home. Sound good?"

"Sure. I'll bring the wine, even if it doesn't go well with pizza."

"How about beer? The Brown Bear pale ale you liked the first night you came to town." He wasn't much of a wine lover.

She nodded with enthusiasm. "That's good stuff, so yes. I'm baking brownies today for Ashley, and I'll wrap up a plate for us."

"A way to a man's heart is through his stomach." What a ridiculous thing to say. He shook off the comment, wanting to get back to work on the doghouse before he said something more embarrassing, such as how he looked forward to spending time with her tonight.

"I don't mean to tell you what to do, but don't you think a doghouse is cold and impersonal? Bo is a friendly dog who needs love and more than an outdoor shelter." She didn't so much as blink those captivating eyes but instead scrutinized him while petting Bo's head. The dog soaked up the attention.

"Do you want to keep him?" he asked. What a perfect question to put the burden back on her. He didn't need or want a dog. Even if he did want Bo, he wasn't home enough to take good care of him.

She stared at the sky as if contemplating the question, then her gaze met his. "I wish, but I can't keep him at Ashley's house. She has enough to deal with and is in a lot of pain." She scratched Bo in that perfect place on his rump, and he stretched out to make sure she didn't stop. She laughed good naturedly. "He deserves a warm, loving home."

Bo whined as if he agreed that someone should bring him inside.

Chris let out a long sigh. "Not fair. You two are teaming up against me."

Bo barked.

"Oh, all right. Now I feel guilty." Bo jogged over to him and licked him on the cheek. "And you, Brittany Adams, have a way of talking me into decisions I don't want to make."

She flashed him a sympathetic grin, melting his resistance like a warm day affecting an icicle. Not even his ex-fiancée had held the power to sway his decisions and confuse his thoughts like Brittany.

"My concern is that I'm barely home, and this guy deserves a family to love him, not a single bachelor who is a workaholic." He ran his hand down Bo's spine, pleased the dog had gained some weight since he started feeding him.

"You are a family, *his* family. You already care about him." She pointed at the dog bowls placed near the back door. Then she nodded at the doghouse. "Or you wouldn't have bought him a shelter."

He remained silent because he had no counter argument.

"Just bring him to work with you in the mornings. He's already used to the area." She gave Bo a scratch behind the ears. "Then home at night so he has a warm house. Dogs make great company. We had one when I was growing up, and I've considered adopting another one."

"Take him." He pointed at Bo, who whined at him and tilted his head.

"See, he's already your dog. No one else can take him."

Chris sighed.

Later that evening, he left work early with a pizza, a case of Brown Bear pale ale, and a dog in the backseat of his truck. If a canine could smile, this one was. He had his mouth open, his lips stretched wide in a grin, and his eyes half shut as if content with life.

The sky resembled steel and the snow-capped mountains made him think of scoops of vanilla ice cream. His stomach rumbled at the thought. Even though he worked in a restaurant, he had forgotten to eat lunch.

When Chris parked by the garage and opened the truck door, Bo jumped out, following him up the back steps and across the deck as if he owned the house. "We're going to head straight to the shower." Bo trotted inside as Chris held open the door. He placed the pizza on the counter, planning to warm it in the oven before Brittany arrived, and set the beer in the fridge.

They made their way upstairs and Chris guided Bo into the shower. He used a combination shampoo and conditioner on him to wash off a layer of dirt and grime. When he finished, Bo shook water all over the bathroom, covering Chris too.

"Hey there," Chris complained, but kept grinning. It was Chris's turn for the shower, and a quick one at that, but he still had to search for Bo.

He found him downstairs … eating the dinner that was once on the counter.

"No! Are you kidding me?" Chris snatched what was left of the pizza and tossed it into the trashcan. "How'd you get that box open anyway?"

Bo licked his lips and watched him without remorse.

"What did I sign up for?"

Bo whined.

"Ugh, okay. Stop eating my dinner or we'll have a problem."

Bo placed his front legs on Chris's chest and gave a playful bark. Just then the doorbell rang. Brittany was here right on time, to the second.

Bo hadn't barked at the doorbell. He followed him to the door as if he didn't know what a doorbell was, which debunked the question of if he had been an inside dog before. When he saw Brittany, however, he started barking. The dog had good taste in women.

Chris led her to the kitchen, but with a long sigh, he explained the dinner problem.

Her face grew serious. "No worries. Can we order one for delivery? Or do you have anything in your fridge I can make?"

Chris shook his head. "Just beer and a tub of chocolate ice cream in the freezer. And of course we have delivery service here in the mountains, but I'll just call ahead to Dog-Tired and have them make us another pizza. We can run up there and get it, but you, Mr. Bo, are going with us." The dog barked in agreement.

Even though he enjoyed Brittany coming over for dinner, he had difficulty getting over Bo eating the pizza.

She raised her eyebrows. "Oh, no. Are you rethinking having Bo here?"

He turned away and nodded.

She tilted her head to the side with pleading eyes. "Can you give him another chance? He's used to scrounging for food, and I'm sure he found the pizza tempting."

Chris shrugged. "We'll see."

When they returned home from Dog-Tired, they ate at the table to keep Bo from climbing into their laps for food. Brittany pushed her plate aside, opening a worn notebook, and wasting no time digging into the details.

"The historic Candlelight Home Tour is in the evening from six to nine. We will hand out flashlights to the guests and ask each homeowner to have an array of battery-operated candles to safely set the ambience of their home."

Chris had seen people walking around at night while carrying flashlights in years past but hadn't been inside any of the homes during the events, so he was clueless about expectations.

"I'm not good at decorating for Christmas," he said as he took a large bite of pizza. There was probably more work involved in getting his house ready than Brittany realized.

"No worries. I excel at decorating."

"What's the reason for having the event at night with candles? Is it history related?"

Her face glowed when he mentioned history. "Oil lamps were often used as a light source, especially in rural areas, but electricity became increasingly accessible in the late 19th and early 20th centuries. Using candles reflects on an earlier period and offers an intimate, cozy holiday ambience. I just love Christmas."

He tried not to scowl.

"Apparently the houses play festive Christmas music and offer themed appetizers." She looked down to read off her list. "Maybe serve small pumpkin or apple cake slices, or offer savory appetizers such as a charcuterie board with bruschetta, cheese, vegetable crudités with dips."

His expression turned dazed.

"According to Ashley, Daisy's Gift Shoppe offers preserves, and she makes homemade pies to order."

"Okay, sign me up for desserts. I'll see if Daisy can make pound cake that can be cut into small squares and topped with preserves." He felt far outside his comfort zone and didn't adapt to change easily, but he agreed to this event, so he might as well go along with Brittany's ideas.

"Wonderful." She wrote something down in her notebook. "What do you need help with to get the house ready?" She glanced around as if assessing its condition.

"Everything." He waved his hand to include the entire house. "I need to repaint the living room, kitchen, and dining room, refinish the hardwood floors, or at least polish them, and put up Christmas decorations."

"I can help you with some of that, like painting and decorating." She glanced up at his least favorite painting in the house, an old, ugly flower arrangement in a vase. "Are you in love with that? At my antique store, I have a perfect oil painting of a horse and carriage on the streets of a mountain town that resembles Snow Valley."

He studied her with interest. "How much and how would I get it here?"

They talked price and he didn't balk at the number. "It's in good condition, and I can have Nancy ship it here if you'd like. We have plenty of time, and it would complement your living room well." She took out her phone from her purse, scrolled through several photos, and showed him a picture of the painting.

"I swear that's this town." He felt drawn to buy the artwork. What an honor to have such a beautiful piece hang on a wall in his house. He studied the painting, mesmerized by the vivid detail and busy everyday life of people who lived in a different era than he. "Can you send me the photo?"

"Sure, what's your cell number?"

He gave her his number, figuring it was good for her to have since they'd be working together on his house.

His phone dinged but she continued to type on her phone before she glanced up at him. "Nancy can ship it out tomorrow. Also, I realize your schedule is busy but let's make an appointment to start painting the walls. That's quite a job."

"Are you always so efficient?" He jutted his chin at her in stubborn defeat. He was financially committed now in this event.

"Of course. That's why I'm a successful business owner."

Ouch. He was also successful, and he didn't procrastinate when it came to his business. "I should have done this a long time ago, but I'll call my friend, Jimmy, to paint the walls. We can handle the trim, polishing the floors, and decorating."

"Sounds like a plan. When can we get started?"

He didn't respond, his mind overwhelmed by the speed of such a commitment.

She wrote something else in her notebook, then turned her attention to him. "If you have supplies, how about tomorrow morning?"

He grimaced. He'd rather work at Dog-Tired, but he'd take what came his way. "I don't keep painting supplies readily available in my shed, as you can see." He pointed to the faded walls. "But I can stop by the hardware store. It's a drive, though, so why don't we start the following morning?"

Bo stood and sniffed, catching a whiff of pizza as Chris opened the box for another piece.

"You want seconds, Bo? Wasn't the first pizza enough?" Chris asked, taking a bite that amounted to almost half the slice.

The canine barked and Chris and Brittany laughed.

"Bo has a dynamic personality. I think you'll be happy with your choice to adopt him." Brittany patted Bo on the head. "That's right, boy. You deserve to live in the house and be someone's beloved pet."

Bo barked again as if understanding her.

Chris grew silent.

He pushed aside the pizza box, making a note to put the leftovers in the refrigerator instead of leaving the container on the counter as he normally did. "Sleeping tonight will be interesting, as well as bringing Bo to the restaurant during the day. But I feel bad letting him roam around town while I work, especially since it's colder outside."

"True. Maybe finish setting up the doghouse so he has a warm place to hang out? You could always fence in the small yard behind the building."

"This dog is starting to get expensive," Chris grumbled. "What we do for animals."

"That's the right spirit." She shoved the notebook into her purse and pushed away her chair. "I need to get back to Ashley, but I look forward to helping you with your house."

"What do I owe you for the help?"

Her forehead wrinkled. "Nothing? I'm doing this for you and Ashley."

"Thanks, but curious … how will you have time to paint trim when you came up here to help Ashley?"

"That won't be a problem because I can run to her house several times. I just remembered she has surgery the day after next, so she will need me. We'll have to start painting tomorrow."

He rubbed his beard, thoughtfully. "Fine. I'll head to the hardware store first thing in the morning, and we can get started when I return. We need to work around Ashley's surgery, of course."

"Do you have an old shirt I can borrow? I didn't pack anything to paint in except a well-worn pair of sweatpants."

"I can dig up something." Chris looked forward to working next to her all day long and seeing her dressed in casual clothes was a bonus. He had to fight off a grin at the thought and walked her to the front door. "Drive safely. The roads freeze up and it's dark out there."

CHAPTER SIX

Sexy thoughts of Chris radiated through my mind as I headed back to Ashley's. Focus! Enough already, no more daydreams about the mountain man who remained off-limits to me.

I strained to see where exactly the turnoff was to Ashley's snow-covered road but the streaked windshield from the weather made it harder to see. I added a squirt of wiper fluid like I always did on cold mornings at the beach, but my wipers left behind a frozen mess. I squinted to see the road.

Ashley's street sign glowed in my headlights, but I misjudged the sharp turn. My tires slid. I overcorrected the steering, and the car hit a patch of ice. I clipped a bank of snow on the right side of the road, the impact jolting me. The vehicle landed in a narrow ditch. With my hand shaking, I shifted the gears into reverse but the wheels spun, not letting me move forward or backward.

I sat stunned for a moment, only my headlights illuminating the dark road ahead of me. No one passed by, and the area was desolate. Ashley was in no position to help, and I knew no one in town besides Chris. I pulled up his name on my phone, grateful he had given me his cell number.

"Hello?" he said with hesitance, and I realized he hadn't entered my information in his phone.

"This is Brittany."

Dead silence. Either he was trying to figure out why I was calling him so soon, or he realized I needed help.

"You won't believe what happened," I said, filling the awkward space between us. "My car slid into a ditch as I turned onto

Ashley's road." I didn't want to ask him for help, but I had no choice unless I called emergency roadside assistance, if they were even available.

"Be right there. Hang tight."

Click.

I turned off my lights and engine but turned on my hazards. The blinking amber lit up the trees with synchronicity. Small tuffs of snow covered the branches of pine trees and other green foliage. The picturesque scene reminded me of a Christmas movie, pretty but deafening quiet except the click click of the hazard lights. I felt embarrassed that Chris had to come save me.

It didn't take long for a beam of light to illuminate the shadowy, wintery scene. A truck pulled up behind me, and a bearded Chris dressed in a ski coat and knit hat walked up to my car. I jumped when he rapped on my window, the noise a stark difference from the deafening peace that had surrounded me. I opened the door and greeted Chris with the utmost appreciation. Bo barked with joy at me from the truck.

"Let's get you out of here, but first, do you have supplies and a blanket in your car as I had suggested you get?" A bellow of breath swept into the air as he talked.

I remained silent for a moment, glancing up and blinking my eyelashes with innocence. "About that."

"Please listen to me. I've lived here for years, and this is your wake-up call." He pointed at my car. "What if you'd been on one of the mountainous roads by yourself without cellular service?"

"For one, I wouldn't be driving at night in the mountains on icy roads. And for two, I'll pack the supplies first thing in the morning." How could he argue with that?

"You never know. People get stuck out on the curvy roads in the daytime too. You can't play too safe around here."

Was he being protective? The fact he cared about me filled me with warmth on this frigid night. Thankfully, he had loaned me his coat, but I wasn't wearing the scarf or hat I had bought. Lesson learned.

I climbed from my car and stood at a safe distance and watched. Chris got busy hooking a chain to my vehicle then hopped back into his truck. The engine revved and mine groaned. My pitiful car jolted a couple of times, but sure enough, he was able to pull it backward until it sat on the icy road. Shivering, I got back in my car to wait for him to finish.

Chris walked up to my window. I slid it down, and he leaned toward me, his hulky body filling the opening. His warm breath danced across my cold cheeks.

"Be careful driving and take the turns slowly. Don't stop on hills and pump the breaks when you come to stop signs." His voice sounded deep, masculine, yet soft and gentle.

I held my breath. The intimacy between us became intense, and for a moment I thought he might kiss me. Not moving, I inhaled a breath and took in his woodsy cologne. The temptation to touch his lips with mine became overwhelming.

He pulled away and stood, tapping the window frame with a quick thud. "Have a good night and tell Ashley I hope she feels better soon. We miss seeing her at Dog-Tired."

His abrupt movement and the mention of Ashley shook me out of my stupor. What had I almost done? My cousin might be in love with the one man who made my pulse quicken at a dizzying pace.

"Have a good night, Brittany." He gave a quick nod and strode off toward his truck, not pulling away until I started up the hill toward Ashley's house.

Breathe. The almost kiss was too much to imagine, and a wave of guilt overcame me. My cousin asked if I'd help her with the tour in general. She didn't intend for me to start having feelings for Chris.

I walked through the front door and into the living room. She was watching a holiday love story, and call it horrible timing, but as I entered the room, the actors enjoyed their first romantic kiss. Another wave of guilt flooded me, and I decided it was time to discuss Chris again to get a better feel for her thoughts.

I opened my mouth to speak, but she interrupted me.

"There you are!" She paused the movie and shifted on the couch, albeit painfully, to face me. "How did it go with securing Chris's involvement with the tour? Did you talk about changes he'd need to make to the house, decorating, and food choices? I'm so excited to have his home on the tour."

My mind whistled like my grandmother's teapot, ready with hot water and to be removed from the burner.

"All is good, and he's agreed. He only wants to include the downstairs, which is fine, but the main rooms require maintenance and updating. It'll be a lot of work but I can help." Spending so much time with him would prove difficult. Even if Ashley wasn't in love with him, the long distance between our homes was reason enough not to get involved with him. "Let's talk about Chris."

"He's my favorite topic. What do you want to know?" Ashley's face lit up with joy just at the mere mention of his name.

"Never mind." Ashley's reaction revealed everything.

"Are you avoiding conflict as usual?" Ashley crossed her arms, scowling with her brows furrowed. "Is there something you want to ask me?

"Are you in love with Chris?" There, I faced my fear of conflict and always wanting to keep peace.

She blushed and smiled. "No, I'm not."

Chris returned home, Bo leading the way to the back door. "You love living here, don't you?"

Woof. Tail wag.

He rubbed behind the dog's ears and ran his hand down Bo's back. "You better be a good boy tonight in the house."

Bo tilted his head.

"That's right. No digging in the trash can, no scratching anything, and no pooping inside." He said it in a lighthearted tone, but his concerns were justifiable.

The following morning, he woke up to a lump next to him. Chris stretched, and in his confused, early morning state of mind, he reached out to the snoring form lying next to him.

"Bo?"

The canine half opened his eyes.

When Chris had gone to sleep, Bo was resting on a rug beside the bed. He hadn't noticed when the dog had jumped up during the night but didn't mind too much, although he wasn't thrilled with dog hair on his comforter.

"Good boy." Bo stayed in bed when Chris got up and showered. When he walked to his closet, the dog watched with interest. Chis finished dressing without Bo's gaze ever diverting.

"Let's go see if my house is still in one piece." He suspected it was, and optimism was important.

He tapped his leg to call Bo, who followed him downstairs. "No damage in the living room." They entered the kitchen and found the trash can still bearing its lid. "I can handle owning a dog if you continue to behave like this in the future."

Bo whined and then barked.

Chris put a K-cup into the coffee machine. "My morning routine isn't anything special, boy."

Routine it was until a squirrel, holding a large nut, perched outside the glass door leading to the deck.

Bo went wild in a barking frenzy. He charged forward and ran smack into the glass, leaving him dazed.

"Are you okay? I didn't think the windows were clean enough to be invisible."

Chris wanted to let Bo outside to use the bathroom, so he didn't have a mishap in the house, but he didn't think the poor squirrel stood a chance of escape. To distract him, Chris took a handful of dog food from the bag, having no idea how much to feed Bo. Guessing at portions served him well as a cook when Doug called out sick and back when he'd first started the restaurant.

But in the morning at home, scrambled eggs were Chris's daily breakfast choice.

Bo glanced up after finishing his dog food, only to beg for the remnants of eggs that Chris hadn't eaten yet. The dog tilted his head, his big begging brown eyes difficult to resist.

"Fine. You can have the scraps." Now he knew why people talked to their animals. He placed the plate on the floor for the dog to lick clean. "Bo, I'm dropping you off at the restaurant while I run to the hardware store for paint and supplies before Brittany shows up."

Woof.

"Let's go." He tapped his leg, and Bo ran outside onto the deck, sniffing the boards like crazy. Thankfully the squirrel was nowhere around. Bo ran into the yard. As always, Chris paused to inhale the cool mountain air, drawing in the fresh pine scent and appreciating the crest of the Blue Ridge Mountains off in the distance. He used to make a point of taking early morning hikes to the top to watch the sunrise, but lately he had lost himself in work.

When had he become such a workaholic?

Within five minutes, he dropped Bo off behind Dog-Tired, then greeted the staff before he left for the hardware store. It surprised him how much he looked forward to seeing Brittany today, even if they planned to paint trim. That was his least favorite part of painting, but he'd bet that spending time with her would help the situation.

Last night had been amazing, and he was glad she had called him to pull her out of the ditch. He hadn't minded and even enjoyed helping her. What surprised him most was when he'd bent down near the window to doublecheck if she had emergency supplies in her car. The intensity between them sparked like a chain against pavement. He wondered if he had imagined the chemistry between them, though. They both had mentioned not wanting to date anyone. Plus, she lived at the beach and had her own life to get back to.

He thought of the adage that the heart wants what the heart wants, but he wouldn't go that far. What he felt was simple chemistry between a man and a woman. That was all. Completely normal.

Chris collected the supplies and paint, and in record time he pulled up in his driveway. Brittany wasn't there but it was still early. The slight disappointment he felt surprised him, but he distracted himself from thinking about her by carrying in the supplies.

As she had the previous night, Brittany pulled into the driveway exactly to the minute. How did she plan out the arrival time with such precision? On a normal day he was either too early or about fifteen minutes late. No matter how hard he tried, he was never exactly to the minute.

The doorbell rang and his heart beat a little faster.

He didn't want this attraction to her. Getting broken up with before the wedding took a toll on his trust and belief in love. Add that to the fact relationships took a tremendous amount of effort and time, which neither of them had. He needed to snip off any budding blooms right now.

She stood on the covered front porch looking like a ray of winter sunshine, dressed in a chocolate brown sweater, complementing the reddish tint of her hair perfectly, and fitted jeans.

He opened the door, letting her breeze in with a smile.

"You are here to paint, right?"

Her brow drew into a straight line, and she tilted her head sideways. "Um, yes? That's what we planned to do today, unless I'm mistaken."

He pointed to his faded T-shirt and torn jeans. "I'm dressed in slum clothes to work, but you look beautiful, as if you are going on a coffee date."

She barked out a laugh. "Hardly. If you think I'd go on a date in these old rags, then you are mistaken. I don't know why I packed them, but something told me I might get down and dirty. Unless you have that old T-shirt you promised me."

He grinned, and she playfully whacked him on the arm. "Right, the T-shirt."

"Get your mind out of the gutter." She laughed so hard she snorted.

Chris laughed. How endearing, refreshing … she was different than anyone he'd ever met.

She glanced around. "Where's Bo?"

"I dropped him off to make his rounds at the restaurant as usual, so he doesn't knock paint cans over or get into anything."

A quick frown crossed her face. "Guess that makes sense."

"Be right back." He jogged upstairs to retrieve a white T-shirt with a sketch of a man fishing in a mountain stream, holding a rod with a large fish attached to the line. He grinned, picturing her wearing a fishing shirt.

When he returned downstairs and handed it to her, the humor on her face delighted him. She changed in the bathroom and returned. The tingling sensation running through his body pleasantly surprised him. No woman had ever worn any of his clothes, and he rather enjoyed the experience of seeing her in one of his shirts.

He offered her a bottle of water to stay hydrated and they got to work pouring paint into plastic cups.

She watched him with interest. "Aren't you concerned about getting paint on the floor? My dad always pours the paint outside."

He shook his head. "That's what drop cloths are for. And the cups are perfect because you don't have to wash them and can throw them away when you're finished."

Brittany stared at him. "You have painting figured out. I've never thought about simplifying the clean-up. What about taping the trim?"

He shook his head. "I never tape. It's a waste of time, and I could have one wall of trim done before I finish taping."

Brittany chuckled. "I can see you are an expert on time-management skills, and I value your insights, but I'm not sure my hand is as steady as yours."

He shook his head. "I'd say you're the expert on time management, not me, but don't stress about painting. The painters will come behind us, so no worries."

"Okay, if you say so. But don't say I didn't warn you." She turned away from him and climbed the step stool, carrying a cup and a paintbrush in hand, looking irresistible in his T-shirt.

"I try to shave off extra work whenever possible," he explained. "That's what happens when you don't have enough hours to accomplish everything you want. It's a never-ending cycle."

"I own a business too, but I don't work constantly. I'm a firm believer in a joyful, work-play balance."

He swallowed hard before he spoke. "I don't relate or know what you're talking about."

She swiped a portion of the crown molding but glanced down at him before she reloaded her brush. "A house project is a perfect way to slow your life down and to change your mindset."

"You're wanting to change me already." His voice sounded deep.

She stopped mid-stroke. Keeping her eyes focused on her work, she said, "Change isn't always a bad thing. It's not like we're an old married couple, set in our ways." Brittany dipped the brush in the paint but flashed him a lopsided grin. "Not even close."

For some reason her comment felt like rejection. Which shouldn't matter. He didn't want to marry her or even date her.

"You can say that again." He climbed a short ladder and got to work, but not without noticing her shocked expression. With a smirk, he began to paint.

CHAPTER SEVEN

The following morning, I woke up early to chirping birds and plentiful sunshine pouring through the frosty windows of my bedroom.

As I drifted in and out of sleep, pleasant thoughts wafted to Chris. Not one to think of painting trim as a fun activity, I had to admit that I appreciated spending time with him yesterday. We'd finished sooner than we expected, so he returned to work for the dinner rush, and I went home to Ashley.

Today was her surgery in the next town over. She was nervous but I suspected she'd start feeling better in a couple of days when her shoulder began healing correctly.

I snuggled deep into the covers, not wanting to get up yet. The sheets were warm from the baking sun, but the bedroom air was chilly. My phone alarm went off, so I stretched my arms above my head, groaned, then counted to three and threw off the covers to start the day.

Once dressed, I poked my head into Ashley's room. "Rise and shine." A morning person she wasn't.

"Who would've thought getting out of bed was so unrewarding?" Her voice sounded groggy and deep.

Ashley needed assistance with her morning routine, but at least the doctor gave her permission to allow her arm to dangle while showering. I helped with her shirt, but she was able to pull on her loose sweatpants.

"I'm becoming adept at being more creative," she said, trying to squirt toothpaste on her toothbrush one-handed.

Her pain level remained unbelievable, and my heart went out to her. Other than empathy and physical help, I didn't know how else to support her other than to assist however possible.

We made the trek through the frozen mountains, and I had flashbacks of my car sliding into the ditch the other night, so I took extra care in driving. It was a relief when we arrived safely. At least the surgery center was closer than I thought possible to a rural mountain town.

While Ashley was in surgery, I took the opportunity to call my best friend Nancy, who was managing my store.

"How are things going? Is business steady, and do you need additional help?" I felt anxious about being away from Time-Worn Treasures for such a long period. It was a first.

"Business is fine. Don't worry about anything," Nancy reassured me. "And I sold the Victorian mantel cuckoo clock with a pocket watch for asking price."

"Fantastic! I'll give you a bonus for selling those beautiful pieces." I had the clock priced a bit on the high side, but anyone who knew clocks would understand its value. I also offered a slight discount if someone bought the two pieces together due to their association to each other. What a surprise finding the watch in a secret compartment had been. "Your news has made my day, maybe even my month."

The clock smelled of old wood and reminded me of visiting my great-grandmother's house when I was a young kid. I used to stare at the cuckoo clock hanging on the hallway wall, waiting for the little bird to slide out and sing. The comforting tick tock mesmerized me as did the swaying pendulum. As always, I considered keeping the rare finds for my own antique collection, but I was in business to make a profit, not to keep the prizes.

The morning cruised by as I worked on my laptop in the waiting room, trying to catch up on the paperwork for the shop. Once Ashley and I returned to her house, my empathy for my cousin grew.

"I'm pitiful," she said, barely able to keep her eyes open. "At least I'm not in pain, thanks to the medication."

"That's a relief. Can I get you anything to drink or eat?"

She curled up on the couch, and one-handedly she pulled a soft, fuzzy blanket over her legs. Her arm remained in the sling. "Sure."

Before I started making a late lunch, the doorbell rang. Ashley's neighbor, Billi, stood at the front door with a casserole in hand. "All you need to do is warm it up in the oven. How's Ashley?"

"She's a trooper," I said with pride. My cousin never complained, never asked for much, and made the best out of a bad situation.

"Let me know if you need anything. We have her on the prayer list at church, and our book club has her on the food chain. Fran is baking lasagna tomorrow, and Kay is making chicken soup and biscuits the following day."

"Thank you so much, but please, don't overwhelm yourselves. Even every other day will be nice." Friends made the world a nicer place, and Ashley had a great support system. Small towns were wonderful, but I suddenly realized that I didn't have the same kind of network back home. I had given Chris a lecture about work-play balance, which I thought I had until I experienced Ashley's friendship circle. My weak support system indicated the necessity to work less and make a lot of new friends. I spent most of my evenings alone, at home, relaxing.

Billi gave me a hug that I didn't realize I needed. The embrace felt comforting, and I soaked up the friendly love.

"Thank you. All of you are so kind to help Ashley." After Billi left, Ashley's cell phone started ringing. She was asleep, so I answered each call and filled her friends in on her progress.

Then my own cell phone demanded my attention. I glanced at the caller I.D., surprised to see Chris's name flash across the screen. We exchanged greetings, made light small talk for a moment, and then he said, "We've got problems."

I waited for him to continue but he didn't. "What kind of issues?"

He exhaled into the phone. "For starters, the painters cancelled. The company is owned by a friend of mine. Apparently, they can't get started for two more weeks, possibly three, but then Thanksgiving falls in there somewhere, so we might be looking at a longer delay."

"That's problematic since the Candlelight Tour is in just over four weeks."

Silence. "That's what I'm saying. I don't think I can be involved in the event."

"Oh, no. That's not going to happen," I said with strong determination. We'd had two additional people sign up for a total of six houses, but we needed Amelia House to make an impressive impact.

"It's too much trouble and not enough time."

"Worst-case scenario, I'll help you paint the walls. I've done it before." Only if she counted painting a guest bathroom and she'd had to repaint it because it turned out streaked, but she didn't dare tell him those details.

He sighed into the phone. "Britt, painting a living room and hallway is a significant undertaking."

Chris had never called me Britt before, but I rather liked the nickname. Hearing him say it made my body tingle. I glanced over at Ashley, snoring on the couch, and guilt crept in once more. I needed to focus on helping him, as well as Ashley, and not allow any feelings between us to develop.

"Let's move forward with the Candlelight Tour," I suggested. "Things will work out. There is an estate sale I want to attend on Saturday if Ashley is feeling better enough to stay home for a few hours. I'd like you to come with me. I usually find treasures, and it's a wonderful way to add antiques to your house without spending a lot of money. I've come across great deals."

"Guess it wouldn't hurt to spruce up my place, even if I don't do the event."

I didn't appreciate how he talked about backing out after making a commitment. "One day at a time."

"See you Saturday, and I'll pick you up." His voice sounded lighter than at the beginning of the conversation, so maybe he was coming around.

Ashley's phone rang again, but this call was from her work. I picked it up with some hesitance.

"This is Brittany," I said. They knew she'd had surgery today, so perhaps they wanted to check on her.

"Hi, I'm Joan, and I am the manager at Event Magic. How's Ashley doing?" Her voice sounded pleasant enough, but my nerves perched on edge.

"She's sleeping soundly." I chuckled as I glanced at her. Her free arm sprawled above her head, one leg dangled from the couch, and she snored like my grandaddy had after a long day of working outside.

"That's good to hear, and I'm glad she's recovering." Joan paused, and tension grew. "We are running out of time to enlist homes on the tour. We only have four."

"Actually, two more signed up." I felt compelled to say this to possibly save Ashley's job, and I hoped Chris would stick with our agreement.

"Really? What two owners?"

I drew in a long breath and exhaled it before I committed myself. "The Langleys and Chris Hart." The only reason for using his full name was to keep emotion from bubbling up and revealing my feelings toward him. The last thing I wanted was to hurt Ashley in any way.

"Wait a minute. Chris Hart?"

"Yes." Another wave of guilt overcame me, but this one felt like dishonesty instead. What if he backed out like he'd mentioned earlier? I glanced at Ashley and knew she deserved the credit for signing up Chris for the Candlelight Tour. Not me. She had a job to protect. "Ashley was able to convince him of the benefits."

What was one little lie to protect my cousin?

It wasn't really a lie, so to speak, but perhaps a slight exaggeration. I just needed to keep him from changing his mind.

No pressure there.

"I'm impressed," Joan said with sincerity in her voice. "I coordinated a small team to help with efforts on the Candlelight Tour. I understand that you're helping Ashley, so let's meet tomorrow at Dog-Tired. Do you think she can attend?"

I glanced at Ashley, who hadn't moved. "She just had surgery, but we can see how she feels tomorrow. Either way, I'll plan to be there."

"Great. Keep me posted."

We agreed on when to meet, and after I hung up, the pressure inside me started building. I didn't mind driving up here to help, but I hadn't realized the required level of my involvement with her work.

The following day Ashley slept a lot. I attributed her drowsiness to the anesthesia but at least she wasn't in much pain thanks to the nerve block.

After she struggled one-handed to feed herself breakfast, I asked, "Are you up for attending today's event meeting?" It burned me up that her boss held expectations of a sick or hurt employee. Then again, I wasn't even an employee, yet Joan wanted me to attend a meeting. Either way, I hoped they asked someone else to take charge of the Candlelight Tour so Ashley could recover in peace.

"Not really. I'm so tired I just want to sleep." Her voice sounded shaky.

"Then that's what you should do. I'll cover for you." We went over Ashley's notes, questions, and suggestions for me to present to Joan and the newly assigned team.

I pulled in front of Dog-Tired five minutes early to keep from getting anxious. Excitement swirled inside me to see Chris at the restaurant, and I tried to squelch the unwanted feelings. From my experience, long distance relationships were difficult and hadn't worked out for me in the past. It was easy to start out with enthusiasm, calling each other every night, but then life took over and one missed day of talking led to another. Before long, the relationship would erode.

I held no desire to experience heartache again.

Not only to spare Ashley's feelings, but to protect my own, I needed to block any romantic thoughts about Chris Hart from my mind. Starting now.

I asked the hostess to lead me to Joan and followed her to a table where three women waited. Once I sat down, we made introductions. Virginia wore her brown hair long and seemed as sweet as her name, and Lynda dressed in a soft, natural colored alpaca sweater with a pale blue accent to match her eyes. Joan sat ramrod straight, her intensity seemingly more of a personality trait than having anything to do with the Candlelight Tour.

We ordered lunch and discussed the event in detail.

"Thanksgiving is less than two weeks away, and the Candlelight Home Tour is just over four. That's not a lot of time," Joan said, taking a sip of coffee. "We appreciate Brittany's help, but we all need to chip in." She flipped open her notebook and began to rattle off the tasks left to accomplish. She started to assign duties to us, including Ashley, which is when I stopped her.

"Is Ashley taking sick days?" I knew the answer to the question but tried to ask politely, so Ashley didn't experience any negative consequences. "She's a committed employee but isn't up for helping right now. Is there someone else who can take charge of this event?"

Joan stared at me. I wasn't trying to be confrontational, but this woman was starting to irritate me.

I sat with the silence, resisting the urge to fill in the quiet. Let her feel awkward because her expectations were unreasonable.

Virginia leaned toward me. "How is Ashley doing after her surgery?"

"I left her sleeping, which she's doing often. But her shoulder isn't hurting near as much … until the nerve block wears off. Her shoulder was shattered and broken in three places." The women cringed and Joan glanced away. I made it my mission to give Ashley as much credit as possible in case Joan had thoughts of replacing her in the future, hence the only reason I had taken on the brunt of responsibility so far.

"Let's talk about security," Joan mentioned as she leaned back in her chair. "We will have extra lighting for the parking lots, shuttles running so people can park in Mr. Daniel's field, and we are encouraging visitors to carry flashlights. We will have them for sale at the sign-up tent when they purchase their non-profit tickets."

Lynda calmly said, "That's great. Why don't we take a portion of the ticket price to hand out free flashlights."

Joan frowned. "I don't think free flashlights are justifiable this year, and it's an added expense. People can bring their own or buy them."

Lynda exuded peace, so Joan's remark didn't frazzle her. In a calm voice she changed the subject. "Before Ashley fell and broke her arm, she had set up the Historical Preservation Award as well as the Community Spirit Award."

"What are those?" Virginia asked as a young man with the most gorgeous brown ringlets tinged by golden highlights placed our food on the table. Tim, his nametag read.

I knew enough about the awards to answer. "The Historical Preservation Award is a special category for homeowners who do an outstanding job showcasing the historical significance of their property. The Community Spirit Award is to acknowledge a homeowner or business who has strived to engage in community participation as well as capturing the essence of holiday cheer. Both awards offer two hundred dollars to the first-place winners as well as a fifty-dollar gift card to Daisy's Gift Shoppe."

Chris walked up and overheard the incentives. He raised his eyebrows and whistled. "That entices me."

Joan whirled around in her seat. "I hear Ashley convinced you to join the Candlelight Tour this year. I'm impressed."

He glanced at me and picked up on my tiniest nod. "She sure did. That's one special lady you have working for you. Too bad she's had a streak of bad luck, but she'll be up and going as soon as possible."

I appreciated that he understood the situation with Ashley's job. We seemed in tuned with each other. I hadn't experienced such a connection with any other man I'd known.

Joan dove into her food without comment, but the more she heard compliments about Ashley, the better. I was now on a quest to make Ashley irreplaceable.

CHAPTER EIGHT

After our lunch meeting dispersed, Chris approached me with an interesting idea.

"I have an old servants' quarters behind my house and haven't been inside in years. Yesterday I went out there and did a fast scan of the place. There's some old furniture that we might be able to use to decorate the house for the Candlelight Tour."

I squealed, envisioning a packed room full of valuable antiques. "I'd love to stop by."

"That's only if you have time and if Ashley doesn't need you. But I'd love for you to look."

"Since we are going to the estate sale tomorrow, it makes sense to see what you have first. I'll text you to see if I have time later today. Are there lights in the quarters?" I hoped so, because the sun set early, and I couldn't wait to see the furniture.

"Yes, but I'll have to wait until after the dinner rush," Chris said, his eyes glimmering with excitement. The way he studied me made my pulse speed up. Avoiding romantic feelings toward him would be difficult.

I left Dog-Tired to make a quick stop at the grocery store. When I entered the front door with my arms full of bags, Ashley took a few of the lighter ones with her free arm.

"Look who's awake. How do you feel?"

She followed me into the kitchen to set the groceries on the countertop. "Much better. I'm still not experiencing a lot of pain, so maybe the nerve block has yet to wear off." She peeked into the bags to see what I bought and pulled out the bananas. "Can you peel this for me?"

I did as she asked and handed the banana back. "Glad you're feeling decent because we need to talk about the meeting today and make solid plans."

She raised her eyebrows. "Went that well, huh?"

I shook my head. "What are your thoughts on Joan?"

Ashley groaned and rolled her eyes. "She's not usually my manager, but since the other woman quit and I inherited the Candlelight Tour, she's been all over me."

"Not surprising. I have concerns about her intentions." I shoved the empty grocery bags into one hanging in the pantry. "I think your job is in jeopardy."

Ashley locked her gaze on me. "Why do you say that? And who would replace me?"

I shrugged. "I don't know, but Virginia and Lynda were at the meeting today too."

"Lynda has always been competitive toward me. She works in the same department as the lady who quit, and she has the same credentials as me." Ashley frowned and threw the peel into the trash. "I don't get it. Can't a person be down with a broken shoulder without the risk of losing her job?"

"Apparently not, but the situation stinks. In the meantime, you might want to talk to your real boss and let him know what's going on."

Ashley rolled her eyes. "Joan and Larry are friends, but I bet he'd listen to me."

We headed into the living room, and I went through the boxes of decorations. I read through the notes then tossed the last notebook onto the table. "There's not a lot here to go on. We shouldn't be required to do any of this since you're taking paid time off."

"True, but if I want to save my job, what other choice do I have?" Ashley sighed and leaned back into the sofa.

"I'll help, but for now you need to rest." I glanced into a box containing flashlights with a folder on top marked *Security*.

Someone had taken detailed notes, and Sam Hanes's contact information jumped out at me. "I'll give Sam a call."

"Tell him you're calling for me. He's a good guy and will answer any of your questions." Her face turned a pale pinkish color.

"Do you have feelings for him?"

"Not at all. He's just nice, that's all."

I wasn't sure I believed her, having seen the same way she looked when talking about Chris.

The rest of the day zipped by. I helped Ashley with meals, changed her sheets, and did laundry. We made a detailed plan for the Candlelight Tour, and I checked in with my friend, Nancy. All was going well at my store. Then I typed a text message to Chris to see if he still wanted to explore the servants' quarters tonight.

Almost immediately he typed back. *See you at seven?*

Will be there.

And watch the icy roads.

I laughed, my mind flashing back to my car in the ditch and our almost kiss. There was the possibility I was wrong and had misperceived the chemistry buzzing between the two of us. A deeper conversation with Ashley was still a must, but I procrastinated by telling myself that she needed to feel better before I brought up the subject.

I wasn't sure where the unpleasant trait of conflict avoidance came from, other than I had to often fight the temptation to people-please.

Perhaps I didn't want to hear the truth if Ashley shared her true feelings about Chris with me.

I held a new respect for driving on snow and icy roads. It took longer to reach Chris's house but at least the trip didn't require a tow from him. As soon as I knocked on the door, he pulled me inside.

"Glad you're here! Let's go out back," he said, more eager to see the servants' quarters than I expected.

"I have to greet Bo first." I ran my hands all over the dog, loving on him while Chris waited patiently. As soon as I finished, Chris whisked me outside.

The moonlight illuminated a long, white building with one window. "Wow, this is bigger than I imagined."

We entered the building, and when he flicked on the light, I drew in a long breath and stared at all the glorious items and furniture. A chill caught me, and I zipped my coat to the neckline. It was a good choice to remember to wear my gloves tonight.

"Why haven't you scoured through all this cool stuff before now? You might have enough to decorate half your house."

"Doubt anything is in decent condition." He picked up an antique oil lamp covered in a thick layer of dust. "This is kind of cool."

I nodded in agreement. "Why don't we make piles of definite keepers, broken items we can repair, and things you don't mind throwing away."

He chuckled at my need to organize. "I understand your interest in digging through all this stuff since you love antiques, but it's rather late in the evening to start a big project. How about we glance over what's here and return in the daylight."

A frown replaced my smile, but I empathized that he didn't want to take all this on tonight.

"If you insist." I reached for a bellow atop a large hope chest and squeezed the handles together. A puff of dust escaped, and I sneezed three times.

He laughed good naturedly. "Who knows how long that's been sitting there."

"Apparently for years." I sneezed again. "But check out this hope chest." I cleared off the top by removing another oil lamp, an ornate frame with a couple staring back at me, and a heavy flatiron once used to press wrinkles out of clothes. It wasn't as though I didn't find those items interesting, because I did, but the hope chest held my attention. I tried to lift the lid, but it only budged the slightest bit. "The hinges must be rusted."

"Here, let me help." Chris reached forward, his arm touching mine.

I paused from the energy pulsating through me, but he didn't seem to notice. How embarrassing to have a one-sided, unwanted crush on a clueless man. This wasn't good for my deflated ego.

He bit down on his lower lip and concentrated on freeing the hinge until the lid opened. "Look at all this stuff," he exclaimed, a visible puff of cold air escaping from his lips.

Excitement swirled through me as I took in the belongings of the chest. "This is more like a treasure chest, except without the gold coins." It was a jackpot for me.

Sitting on top of a stack of linens and quilts was a simple, yet dark wooden music box with a floral hand carving and decorative inlay work. I pulled off my gloves and handled the box with care, realizing it was an antique Swiss music box circa 1840, likely made from walnut. I opened it and swooned.

"Look! The original tune card is on the inner lid. But the scripted writing of the song names is hard to read." I grew dizzy with excitement at finding such a piece.

"I can tell you love your job." He stared at me with a dazed, delicious gaze, as if he found me attractive because I knew such geeky information.

"Love isn't quite enough to describe what I feel. Passion maybe." I turned the winding mechanism, and a stream of soft, tinkling music flooded the room. "It works!"

I felt him press closer to me to take in the music box's features. If he didn't feel this wild chemistry between us, I'd be shocked.

I planned to stick with what I knew, and that was antiques.

Gently setting the music box on a side table, I lifted the stack of blankets and linens and placed them aside. What really captured my attention was a cotton, hand-sewn, sunny-yellow quilt with floral-stemmed blooms.

"During the Great Depression and World War II, they often reused feed sacks to create clothing and quilts to save money," I said with awe in my voice. The collection of items in the quarters seemed to be a mishmash of different centuries. "This would be perfect on any smaller bed you may have." I had yet to check out the upstairs and had no idea what kind of furniture the rooms held.

Excitement lit up his face. "I have just the bedroom for this."

I set it aside in the "keep pile," digging deeper into the hope chest. "Oh! Wait until you see this." I pulled out a notebook filled with family recipes.

"This makes my night, my week, maybe my month!" Chris grinned wide and gave me a warm hug.

His arms felt strong, protective, and I caught a light whiff of cologne.

We both realized what we were doing and pulled away, staring at each other for a prolonged moment.

To break the awkwardness, I handed him the notebook, trying to catch my breath.

He seemed flustered as he paged through the cookbook, and then he lit up like he'd received the best Christmas present of his life. "The recipes are hard to read but I can make them out. This is incredible." He continued to thumb through the worn pages. "Someone wrote about how to use rationed ingredients creatively."

While he studied the recipes, occasionally commenting on which ones he wanted to try, I pulled out the last remaining items in the chest. There was a large cast iron pot and pan, silverware, and plates. Once I finished admiring those objects, I moved away from the chest to study the two side tables I had placed items on. They needed some polishing but would dress up Chris's living room nicely.

"There are recipes in here that use their own vegetables from the garden," he said with admiration. "A lot of casserole staples and even casseroles for leftovers, as well as baked goods. Cookies, pies, and cakes. They used a reduced amount of butter and sugar."

"Those items were rationed during World War II," I said, now studying a simple oak chest of drawers, likely used by the servants. It stood on one side of the window as if stationed in its original location in the quarters.

Chris spoke, pulling me out of my thoughts. "There's a recipe for Southern biscuits. I'm going to try this out." He closed the notebook and held it close to his chest. "What a gift."

Without thinking, I placed my hand on his. "It really is. Just think about how long the treasures were here, waiting for you to find them."

Our gazes met again, lingering.

I turned away and pointed toward the chest of drawers. "This would be perfect for the room with the quilt."

"It's simple but beautiful. I can't believe I never paid much attention to going through these." He glanced around at various items placed on a small dinner table that seemed to belong in the quarters as well. "We've found a lot but not much for the living room. Especially since the Candlelight Tour with be contained to the main floor."

"You could always include the upstairs if you want, but we might find items for the living room tomorrow at the estate sale." The moon shone through the dirty window. I needed to get back to Ashley soon. I started placing the items back into the hope chest, bumping into Chris once more. The way he looked at me with such caring, friendly eyes, and a slight smile, melted my heart.

I fought to keep my composure and resisted leaning forward to kiss him. I'd bet his lips were soft, gentle, and swoon-worthy. To keep myself in check, I backed away.

"Need to go. I'm sure Ashley's waiting for me." I opened the door, ready to run.

"Brittany, are you okay? I hope I didn't do something to make you feel uncomfortable."

Of course, he did. Just being next to him was enough to make me feel uneasy.

"No, no." I reassured him even though it was a stretch of the truth. "I need to get back to Ashley. See you tomorrow morning."

His eyebrows drew together as if he was confused. "I'm looking forward to it. I'll pick you up at seven."

I agreed, waved at him, and high tailed it out of the quarters. When I reached my car, I sat there trying to breathe in slow, deep breaths. I had never experienced such a strong reaction to anyone before. Why now? The one man who my cousin seemed passionate toward, and who lived hours away from me. We both had businesses that neither of us could leave behind.

What would happen if we explored this connection, or if it advanced on its own?

A long-distance relationship was off the table for me, and I absolutely wouldn't sell Time-Worn Treasures. Neither one of us wanted our hearts to break when I had to leave, but that was inevitable.

What was the answer to this problem, and how did we move forward?

CHAPTER NINE

The early morning started like a whirlwind. The nerve block had worn off and Ashley required more help today due to pain, but I didn't mind. I had second thoughts about leaving her alone, but she insisted I go to the estate sale.

"You seem to be spending a lot of time with Chris lately," she said, her head tilted as she sat at the table with a plate of scrambled eggs in front of her.

I didn't know if she based her observation out of curiosity or possibly jealousy.

Ask her!

"About him," I asked, ready to tackle the subject more. "I'd like to know what your real feelings are for him."

She smiled, her eyes taking on that familiar dreamy look. "I think he's the best."

I sat there, not sure how to proceed. *Dig deeper.* "In a romantic way?" There I asked her, and now I waited for the answer I dreaded.

"Chris is a friend, a close one." Ashley rubbed her face as if to block me from seeing her reaction.

"Ashley, I'm not sure what a close friend means. I'm asking because I like him but don't want to disrespect you."

Her jaw dropped. "Do I want romance with him? Of course, I do." She turned away, staring out the window at a towering fir tree. My hopes plummeted as she turned back to me. "But we aren't in a relationship or even dating."

Hearing that my cousin wanted to be more than just friends with him was enough to stop my developing interest out of loyalty to her, but I couldn't make my intensifying feelings for him disappear suddenly. With him, I felt an attraction I'd never experienced before.

What a dilemma.

Bubbly Christmas music filled the awkward silence growing between us.

"How are you spending your morning with him?" she asked with an accusatory edge in her voice.

"We are going to an estate sale to help him decorate his house for the Candlelight Tour." Wasn't that what she wanted, for me to have his house presented with excellence?

"Great! So he one hundred percent said yes to the Candlelight Tour?" She seemed to relax and shoved a bite of eggs into her mouth.

"I'm not sure, but he's making progress. His house requires a lot of work, and the painter he hired bailed at the last minute. I helped him with the trim, but the walls are out of my realm of expertise."

"Understandably so. What will he do about the walls?" She drank her juice, the glass reflecting the morning sunshine.

Chris's truck pulled up out front, not in the driveway since he pulled an enclosed trailer behind him. He tooted the horn. "I've got to run. Call if you need me." I went to the closet and pulled on Chris's warm coat and tugged on my boots and gloves. Once I sat on the front seat of his truck, he leaned in for a quick hug. My world spun for a pleasant moment before Ashley's words flashed in my mind. I pulled away.

"Good morning. Looks like we're going to have a warmer day today," he said. The sun streamed through the windows, making me unzip my coat.

"We could use one. I miss the mild temps of the beach." Funny, though, how I hadn't thought much of beach life since I'd been in the mountains. I had to speak over the loud rock music blasting from the radio to give him the address of the estate sale. "Why aren't we listening to Christmas music?" Then I glanced in the backseat. "Where's Bo?"

He turned down the music. "I brought him to the restaurant to prevent any mishaps in my house. As far as the music goes, I never listen to Christmas music. It brings up complicated memories."

"Care to talk about it?"

He grew quiet. When he spoke, he kept his eyes on the road. "Like I mentioned before, not everyone loves Christmas. A lot of people experience loss, and this time of year is painful for them."

He hesitated and I waited for him to continue.

"Disliking Christmas goes deeper than having Dana end our engagement on Christmas Eve. That was bad enough and painful, but I also don't have family to share holiday meals and everything that goes along with Christmas." He steered around an icy patch, keeping his attention focused until the road became clear again. "Sure, people ask me over to their houses but it's not the same as having my own gathering."

I frowned, wishing his circumstances were different. "No family at all?" That would be difficult to handle, and not just at the holidays.

"None. I've had three sets of foster parents. Don't get me wrong, I'm grateful for each of them but I can't imagine what Christmas as a child would have felt like. I've never sat around the tree opening presents."

I exhaled. "I'm sorry."

He stared ahead at the curvy road. "I'm a foster child, and of the three families I stayed with, none of them celebrated Christmas much. I remember a woman stopping by a couple of times with a present for me, but I never knew who she was." He flipped on his blinker and turned on a narrow mountain road. "I suspect now that she is my mother."

"Has she ever returned?"

He shook his head. I reached out and touched his elbow, but he stiffened so I let go. I felt bad that he didn't want me to comfort him.

"Let's have a Christmas get-together at your house this year." Excitement shot through me at the thought of making his holiday better. "Maybe we can give you what you missed as a child."

He glanced over at me. "I don't know. Let me think about it."

We turned onto another road, rewarding us with wooden fences, snowy pastures, and woods. Scenic mountains hovered in the background.

What a wonderful postcard setting.

My parents popped into my mind, and I wondered how they were doing. They were not prone to texting, especially while abroad, and hadn't reached out to me. I was sure they were having the time of their lives.

"We're here." He pulled the truck onto a rock road bordered by Christmas trees growing in rows on a side of a mountain. A sign out front welcomed us to cut down our own.

"Let's do that!"

A puzzled expression crossed Chris's face as he glanced at me.

"Your house needs a huge round tree by the front window in your living room." I squirmed in my seat, my excitement growing.

He raised his eyebrows. "Isn't it kind of early? Thanksgiving is next week."

"Exactly. It's next week already, so we need to start the holiday preparations." I couldn't wait to decorate his house with him.

"Why bother going to all the trouble when a few weeks later I have to pack everything away? What's the point?"

I stared at him, determined to create new associations with the holiday. "Why do we celebrate anything if it's not for the delight it stirs in us?" I felt guilty as soon as I said the words.

"Let's talk about it later." He parked the truck outside an old house, the yard full of someone's beloved possessions spread out for people to sort through.

Estate sales always brought mixed emotions. The items were someone else's memories, representing prized possessions people had enjoyed during their lifetime, which I found sad and heartwarming at the same time. But I also appreciated the thrill of finding hidden treasures among the remnants of someone's collection.

Even though we arrived early, people started to invade the grounds.

"What are we looking for here to decorate my house?" Chris asked, somewhat subdued. I wondered if it had to do with our Christmas conversation.

"Anything that calls out to you. I'm thinking we need more antique furniture for downstairs." Or any Christmas decorations, but that didn't seem promising after he explained why he didn't like the holidays.

We browsed the items on the tables quickly before making our way into the house. I wanted to catch any good furniture options before others made their way inside. Immediately, I noticed a rocking chair sitting in the corner.

"Look!" I said, trying to keep my voice low so as not to attract the attention of another couple scrutinizing the furniture too.

"You like that?"

"It reminds me of a rocking chair my grandmother used to have in her front room." I glanced at the tag, priced lower than I expected. "If you like this, it's a good deal."

"Let's buy it."

I flagged the woman working. "We'd like to purchase this, but we want to keep looking." She marked SOLD on the tag along with my name, and I thanked her.

"I can tell you have done this a time or two. Would you believe we don't have an antique shop in town?" He glanced at an old-fashioned table holding two large figurines of a man and woman. "I like these too."

"I can't believe no one has tapped into the antique market in Snow Valley. What a shame." I checked the price tag on the figurines and the table. "The table needs fixing up, which isn't an issue other than time involved, but the price is fair. However, the figurines are far underpriced. They are hand-painted, porcelain

European Bisque figurines from the early 20th century. There are slight signs of cosmetic wear, but the price is unbelievably low."

"The figurines would look fabulous in my living room, so let's buy them." He picked up the female statue, a raw tenderness showing in his eyes. "I'll feed you and Ashley dinner for a week at Dog-Tired, anything you want, if you restore this table for me. For some reason it reminds me of my blurry past and brings out an odd sense of comfort in me." He ran his hand gently along the ridge of the table.

My heart practically liquified into a pool of empathy for this man. "Any feeling of comfort is good. If this piece brings that out in you, we should get it. As far as restoration, I'll take you up on dinners for a week." I flagged the same lady, and without asking she marked SOLD on the tags.

"This is kind of fun," Chris said, already eyeing up a coffee table that would look spectacular in place of the dilapidated piece near his couch. "I think we've hit a treasure trove."

"Exactly why I love frequenting estate sales. I've found some amazing deals." I studied the coffee table, somewhat concerned about the price. "I think we need to ask them to come down on this. It's nice but overpriced."

"I'll take your word. You're the antique doctor."

I laughed at his choice of words. No one had ever said anything nicer to me.

We bartered with the woman, but she wouldn't budge on the price. "It's still early and we think it's worth every penny," she said, her voice confident.

After she walked away, I said, "Unless you absolutely love this piece, I think we need to walk. We can try again after we've gone through everything. If it's still here we can always barter again."

"I do love it but agree with your approach."

"Are you okay if we lose it to someone else?" That was a real concern, especially if he had his heart set on owning the coffee table.

"I'm okay with losing it, but it'll hit here a bit." He pressed his hand to his heart, and mine melted like the chocolate he used to make hot chocolate at Dog-Tired. There were those special moments he allowed his vulnerability to show, and I wanted to see more.

"Get it if you want."

"That's okay. I trust the process." He headed to the opposite corner to admire an ornate piano with ivory keys. "That's a beauty but would be difficult to deliver. And where would I put it."

"In the parlor?"

His eyes lit up. He touched the keys, and although the piano was off-key, he played the beginning bars of Beethoven's Moonlight Sonata. It was my favorite piece that my grandmother loved to play on her piano. The joy I saw on his face spoke volumes.

"Wow, I had no idea you could play."

"My foster parents paid for piano lessons. At first, I resisted but then learned I loved playing." He belted out another delightful piece that I was unfamiliar with, but the music captivated my attention.

He was multi-faceted, and his history fascinated me.

"Are you thinking about buying the piano?" I glanced at the price tag. "It's reasonable, likely because most people aren't interested in paying someone to move it."

"I'll consider the possibility and love the idea."

We made our way into the kitchen, but he didn't see anything that interested him there. Then we walked up the steep stairs to the bedrooms. The rooms enveloped me with their cozy quilts, antique headboards, and knickknacks on the mantels. We collected a pile of items, consisting of vases holding old-fashioned flowers, large candles, and a fancy jewelry box. He didn't need these items for the Candlelight Tour, unless he opened the upstairs to the public, but again, the decorations would make the bedrooms feel homey. If they brought him joy, I was all for it.

"Check out this handmade braided rug," I said. Rugs were one of my favorite ways of decorating bedrooms to make them feel welcoming. Plus, I couldn't imagine climbing from the bed and placing my bare feet on a cold, wooden floor on a chilly mountain morning.

"Love that." He picked up the rug and added it to the pile.

"I realize this is a bigger investment than you might have expected, but your home and you will be thankful for the purchases. A home should feel welcoming." At least that was my take, as I had grown up that way between my parents' home and my grandmother's. Some naïve people complain that antiques had a way of making a house feel cold, but not me. And rugs warmed up the room.

From there we headed outside to sort through the tables. Many of the items had already been combed through, but we got the primo finds on furniture, which was well worth the tradeoff.

There were oil lamps, dishes, clothes, and a set of kitchen knives, but nothing stood out to me as a great find until we entered the barn. Another coffee table awaited us, made of solid oak.

Chris whistled under his breath. "I like that better than the one inside." He fingered the price tag. "And it's a lot less expensive."

"That's because it's not as elaborate but it's sturdy. Both would complement your living room, but this one is more masculine, which fits you."

He glanced at me and smiled with those perfect white teeth. "I'm a manly man?"

Heat rushed across my face, burning my cheeks. "Yes, that's exactly what I'm saying."

Chris leaned in close to my ear, and his warm breath tickled my neck. "Believe me, I'm all man," he said with a husky voice.

My pulse quickened. I stood still, barely breathing.

"Don't ever forget." He winked and backed away.

I had no answer.

He flagged an older gentleman over. "We'll buy this. I have several items inside the house too."

"It's a great table and choice." He marked the tag.

I still hadn't found a true treasure, at least not yet. Maybe I was spoiled, but back home I always discovered one special treat at every sale.

The barn held mostly equipment for livestock and horses. My intuition told me this wasn't where gems usually hid, so I left the barn and approached the last table we had yet to browse. I picked through several objects when my gaze landed on a beautiful ivory broach, cameo style, intricately carved with a woman's profile. The detailed high definition of her clothing and hair in a delicate lace style blew me away. I picked it up and another woman rushed over to me.

"Look at this," I said to Chris. "It's tempting to keep it for myself."

"I was considering that broach!" The woman leaned toward me with her arms crossed, scowling.

"Sorry, but it was just sitting here on the table." I turned it over in my hands, recognizing its well-preserved condition. Whoever owned this had taken excellent care of the beautiful piece from the late nineteenth century. Due to international trade restrictions on elephant ivory to curb poaching, ivory broaches were no longer made or sold new anymore. There was no way I planned to allow a rude woman to keep me from buying this valuable piece at such a low price.

She reached for the broach in my hands, but I turned my shoulders to block her. A man walked over. "Is there a problem here?" he asked in a calm voice.

"Yes. I wanted that broach, and she snatched it from me."

"I did no such thing," I said to the woman, keeping my shoulders positioned to block her. "The broach was sitting on the table."

Chris pushed his way between the woman and me. I flashed him a smile of appreciation for acting as my bodyguard, protecting me, and I loved his demeaner that demanded that no one mess with me.

"Well, the lady has it in her hands, so it looks like it belongs to her if she wants to buy it." The man raised his eyebrows to measure my interest in the fabulous piece of jewelry.

"Absolutely, I will buy this." How elegant this treasure was, the find of the day, and one I wished to keep but probably wouldn't. Occasionally, I did like to reward my efforts for what I'd accomplished so far with my business, but this might not be that time.

I bought it straight out, not daring to put a sold tag on this item. My bodyguard stood near, emitting strength and a no-nonsense attitude. My attraction increased tenfold. Oh, boy. I was in trouble now.

CHAPTER TEN

Two men loaded Chris's trailer full of his purchases from the estate sale. He'd never thought of attending one before and found it useful in decorating his house with antiques at an inexpensive price. Had he known this secret years ago his house would have looked vastly different.

He was also glad he brought the trailer to haul off their finds.

On the way out, Brittany stopped him. She pointed across the road at the entrance to the tree farm. "Let's buy a fresh Christmas tree. You won't be sorry," she said, full of excitement. "When I was a kid, my family drove up to the Great Smoky Mountains each year to cut down our tree. Since they're abroad, it seems right to continue the tradition."

He glanced over at her. "Sounds like you had a wonderful childhood." He envied kids who'd had family rituals and made memories together. But he couldn't complain. His foster families had taken decent care of him.

"Let's create those memories for you." As soon as he agreed, she bolted from the truck.

For now, he'd enjoy making holiday memories together. Then she'd return home and all the pleasant new memories he'd made with her would taunt him.

A small log cabin stood in front of them, a fire barrel positioned near the trees, sending a plume of smoke into the blue-mountain sky. Christmas music played from an outdoor speaker declaring it was beginning to look a lot like Christmas. The large white bulbs that hung overhead from one tree to the next gave the spot a festive feeling. Along with the backdrop of the mountains, the scene did look like a romantic Christmas movie.

An older man in coveralls greeted them as they approached. "Welcome to Merry Berry Christmas. Grab a hand saw and cut down the one you like, or you can pick from our selection." He pointed to an area where cut trees leaned against a fence.

Chris flashed Brittany a questioning glance, but she shook her head.

"No way. We need the full experience."

He chuckled at her enthusiasm and took her hand as they headed out to the rows of Fraser firs dotting the hillside. The intoxicating smell of Christmas filled his nose. An old forgotten memory begged for acknowledgement as it gnawed at his fuzzy mind. He barely remembered that same woman visiting, bringing a package containing a truck for him. They sat by a Christmas tree, like what he smelled now. Holiday music played in the background, and he remembered hugging the woman, not understanding who she was or where she came from.

It had to be his real mother.

He shook his head to see her with more clarity, but the memory faded.

"Look at this one!" Brittany stood in front of a large tree. "This is perfect."

He stared up at the towering trunk and laughed, feeling a sense of childlike pleasure. "No way will that fit in my living room."

"You sure?" She grinned so big it warmed Chris's heart.

"They always look smaller outside," he said, as if he were an expert. He'd never shopped for one that he could remember. His last foster parents had kept a plastic one in a bag upstairs in the attic, and each year he'd helped them drag it into the living room. No wonder he didn't like putting up trees. It was normally a lot of hoopla, but he had to admit that today he was having fun.

"You're probably right. We always gauged our tree choice based on my dad's height." She eyed Chris. "How tall are you?"

"Six feet."

"Then you're right. This tree is about three feet taller than you." She giggled, and he caught a glimpse of a younger, carefree version of her as a child.

He found her laugh contagious and impulsively scooped her into his arms, holding her tight. They stared into each other's eyes. She felt right, as if they were meant to be together. Brittany's gaze softened, but then she pulled away.

The moment turned awkward, but he recovered first.

"How about this one?" He pointed to a tree a little taller than him but rounded. He now had a sense of her preference and what she had in mind for his house.

Her serious expression relaxed. "Yes! That will be beautiful in your living room. I can see it decorated with ornaments and ribbons in front of the window."

He had wanted to avoid Christmas, yet here Brittany was, making him face demons of his past. He tried to visualize her description of the tree inside his home but no chance. He'd have to trust her and, so far, she'd been right about everything from the estate sale to choosing a tree.

"This is the one?" He carried the saw in hand, ready to cut.

"Yes, if you approve. After all, it's yours." She smiled so big that he wanted to draw her back in his arms and kiss her for a long time.

"Works for me." He got busy sawing the base of the tree and, before long, it fell with a thud to the ground. "That was actually enjoyable."

"Memories." She grinned at him, and they dragged the tree down the hill to the man in coveralls who watched them with interest. He bagged it for them and helped Chris lift it into the back of the truck and tie it with rope while Brittany warmed her hands over the fire barrel. When the men shook hands, the elder gave Chris a wink and glanced at Brittany.

On the way home they made a pit stop in a nearby town to purchase colored ornaments, light blue ribbon with silver bells that Brittany insisted upon, a tree stand and red skirt.

When they returned to town, they stopped to see if Bo was behind Dog-Tired, and he was. He watched them approach from his new doghouse.

Brittany kneeled and tapped her leg. That was the only invitation Bo required, and he left the doghouse and ran up to her, giving her a long lick across her cheek. "You're such a good boy." She rubbed the dog behind the ears and turned to Chris. "How do you think he'd do if you left him at home during the day?"

Chris crossed his arms. "I think he's fine here. He knows this area, and if I let him run near my house he might get lost."

"Do you think he's ever stayed inside alone? It's supposed to be cold all week."

He frowned. "Doubtful. He does well at night but usually sleeps on my bed with me. He hasn't had any potty accidents, but he did eat our pizza when it was on the counter."

She chuckled and nodded. "That he did. Does it get colder than this during the heart of winter?"

"It does. And snowy too." People didn't flock to this area to ski for no reason. "But I also don't want him to tear up my home."

"That's valid. I don't know how to train a dog to behave in the house."

"I have a dog pen outside, but I'd hate to leave him confined all day when he can run free here." He rubbed his chin. Truth be told, the thought of Bo roaming downtown made him consider the possibility of a car hitting him.

"True, although the pen at home wouldn't be so bad with the addition of a doghouse to keep him safe and warm during the day."

He nodded, watching Bo as he turned his rump toward Brittany to rub.

If something happened to him, he'd blame himself. Perhaps he needed to rethink Bo's living situation during work hours. He hadn't wanted to love this dog, but Bo had a way of sneaking into every crevice of his life.

When they returned home with Bo in tow, Chris called a neighbor to help carry the tree and the furniture into the living room. They brought the items into the parlor and placed them against the far wall, leaving room for a later piano delivery. After small chit chat and goodbyes, the man left them alone to deal with the tree.

"How about some hot chocolate before we start the decorating process?" He knew the answer before he finished asking. She nodded with enthusiasm, and they shared another flirtatious gaze.

The way Brittany's hair dangled on her shoulders, and her sweet smile, made him want to stare at her. He found her beautiful. Inside and out.

Her sunny disposition had begun to thaw out his guarded heart, giving him a hint of a spring morning after years of living in an overcast, frozen life. He glanced down at Bo, snoring on the cushy dog bed he'd bought a few days ago.

"Can I help?" She stepped in close enough to distract him.

"Nope, but I appreciate the company." After he filled two mugs full of steaming hot chocolate, he sprayed a dollop of whipped cream on top and added a hint of nutmeg for a dash of color.

"Looks delicious." She blew on the hot chocolate and took a small sip. A smudge of whipped cream covered the tip of her nose, and they laughed. He wiped it off with his forefinger, resisting the urge to kiss her but not wanting to make her uncomfortable. They still had a tree to set up and decorate.

She paused, as if reading his original intention. "I need to check in with Ashley to make sure she's okay being alone this long." At his nod, she gave Ashley a quick call and then hung up a few minutes later. "All is good. She's been sleeping on the couch and watching Christmas movies, taking it easy. I'd left her lunch and snacks, so she has everything she needs."

They walked into the living room, and Chris lit the candles in the old fireplace. "Wish this chimney could handle a real fire but it's not safe, so candles it is."

"Understandable."

Bo moved his way into the room and sat on the oriental rug near the new coffee table from the estate sale. It amazed him how a few upgrades had made a significant difference to his house.

Brittany pulled up Christmas music on her phone, turning the volume too loud for his taste, and began to sing. He groaned, suddenly uncomfortable with the tunes, with decorating for the holiday, with a tree in his living room. Feelings of inadequacy surfaced within him, making him understand the childhood he'd never had, and the fiancée who'd walked out on him Christmas Eve. An old loneliness hid beneath the surface of his smile. He hoped Brittany didn't notice because she was clearly enjoying herself.

She helped him secure the tree in the stand. "A little more to the left."

He obliged, although he didn't care about the tree being perfectly aligned.

"Nope, too far. A little more to the right."

She repeated the commands a few more times, with Chris adjusting the trunk.

"That's enough, Brittany. No one is going to notice."

"Absolutely, people will." She stepped back, analyzing the tree.

"It's good enough," he said, standing up to stretch.

The tree task highlighted a major difference between them. She preferred perfectionism due to her analytical personality. From what he had observed, her processing skills proved much slower than his. He had always been more of a go-getter, a workaholic, and when he made a decision, which was most often informed but quick, he held fast and didn't budge. People often labeled him as stubborn and told him he didn't take enough time off to relax.

Brittany made herself cozy on the couch and began to unwrap packages of ornaments while Chris hung the lights on the tree. He had to admit, the festive music and atmosphere lightened a mundane chore.

Brittany looped a rope necklace with a jingle bell around her neck, hopping up from the couch to hang a big red ball on the tree, while dancing to the music. She grabbed another one and tossed it at him. "Come on. Help me."

He took the ornament from her, playing with the hook.

"Hang it," she encouraged.

He did so to appease her, but then she handed him one ornament after another. When they finished, a glimmer of holiday cheer bubbled from an unfamiliar place deep inside his soul.

She stood back to admire the tree. "Beautiful! We did a fabulous job, and it brightens the entire room."

He took it all in, and she was right. The white lights reflected off the ornaments, and even the music became tolerable. "My living room has come to life."

She tilted her head forward with innocence and squealed, "I knew you'd love it."

There was something so refreshing and sweet about her. He had to be cautious because, if he wasn't, when she left for home in a few weeks, she'd leave a gaping hole in his heart.

He'd already patched one barely healed hole in his heart and didn't need to make another.

Chris had put everything he had into Dog-Tired, and he wasn't about to relocate. He suspected she felt the same way about her antique store.

But she had revived long-dead emotions.

Brittany clapped her hands together. "Let's stop for today."

"Today? You mean there's more?"

She frowned at him. "Of course. We're just getting started. Is that okay?"

Be honest, even if she gets upset.

"The tree is more than enough for me. Remember, I don't celebrate the holidays, and I'm a bachelor. I don't need all of this …" He spread his arms out wide to include the tree and the room.

"I understand." Her shoulders sagged with disappointment. "I thought we were doing this for the Candlelight Tour."

He sighed. "How much more holiday cheer do we need?"

She tilted her head, an empathetic smile spreading across her face. "Let's just add some greenery and candles to the mantel and call it finished, besides cleaning up the new furniture and finding a place for each item."

"Good deal." He breathed a sigh of relief. Thankfully, she wasn't the type to go overboard with decorating the entire house. The living room he could deal with.

They worked together to clean up the mess of boxes and leftover ribbon on the floor. She said, closing an empty box, "You might want to save these for later, when you take down the tree."

He paused to absorb what she'd said, and then reality hit him. "I hadn't thought this out in full detail. Guess I figured you'd be here to help me put this stuff away in the attic." Cleaning up afterward sounded overwhelming.

She shifted her gaze to him, her eyes sparkling from the twinkling lights of the tree. "Sorry about that. I thought you realized that I'm leaving the day after Christmas."

He frowned. "Then we can take it down beforehand."

Her face fell, deflated by his words. "Before Christmas?"

"We set it up for the Candlelight Tour, nothing more. Isn't that what we agreed on?" He crossed his arms, not liking the intensity of her stare. This was why he'd never agreed to the Candlelight Tour before. It was too much work for a few weeks, without any benefit to him.

"If that's what you want, sure." She stacked the boxes on top of each other. "Where do you want to store these in the meantime?"

He took them from her. "In the attic." Out of sight, out of mind.

Bo followed him upstairs. When he returned, she had her coat and gloves on. "Chris, do yourself a favor."

Silence filled the house. She had turned off the music and the festive mood drained like an overturned kettle of hot water.

"What's that?" he asked.

"Embrace change, confront your inner demons so you can live in the present moment. Without that, you have no happy future." She inhaled a sharp breath, as if the conversation was as difficult for her as it was for him. "Our childhood makes us who we are, but we have the power to let go. You're a great man. Let people in."

He didn't respond. Instead, he stood ramrod straight, attempting to hide all emotion from his face.

"Promise to at least think about what I said."

"Okay, and thanks for everything today. I can't promise I'll embrace change, but I can at least appreciate your wisdom." He inhaled a long breath. "Sounds like you've been there before too."

"I have, but I refuse to be stuck in the past."

Like the antiques she obviously loved. At least she had the insight to understand where he was emotionally, but he'd consider what she said. For himself. He'd spent so many years avoiding pain, but it might be time to release the hurt and heal.

CHAPTER ELEVEN

After I confronted Chris about addressing his inner demons, I couldn't help but notice the flash of raw pain in his expression. Seeing his vulnerable side struck a nerve in me. Maybe the Candlelight Tour was too much for him if decorating a Christmas tree triggered pain.

"He was miserable?" Ashley asked, sitting at the table eating a bowl of cereal with one hand.

"Not when we were at the estate sale, or even cutting down a tree. That was fun." Romantic even, but I wasn't about to admit that to Ashley. "Do you know his history and why the holidays make him uncomfortable?" I didn't want to say too much to protect what little he'd confided in me.

"I know he had three sets of foster parents. None of them seemed to celebrate the holidays much. The last foster parents were kind but older. They had no other kids, and their extended family lived out of state, so other than a meal and maybe an exchange of a gift or two, their holidays remained quiet."

"That explains a lot. I'm not sure how well he's going to handle people meandering around inside his house, snacking, talking, and admiring his home." From what I knew about him already, he was a private person.

"It's too late to pull his house out of the Candlelight Tour." Ashley took the last bite of cereal and pushed her bowl away. "We're already pressed for participants, and the event will be here before we realize. I spent some time on the phone with Sam from security, and we'll have to find different parking for our main lot."

I rubbed the back of my neck to relieve the tension headache beginning to develop. "It's one thing after another. What happened to the main parking?"

She sighed, turning her attention to a bright male cardinal on a branch outside the window. After the bird flew away, she returned her gaze to me with deep creases across her forehead. "Farmer John backed out. With the ground wet from rain and snow lately, he doesn't want his cow pasture turned to mud and filled with tire tracks."

"That's understandable, but what will we do?" I debated if I wanted to take a pain reliever to stop the developing headache before it intensified, or to give it a chance to go away on its own. I wasn't one who took a lot of medication. I preferred the more stress-free life at the beach.

She shrugged. "I don't know."

"Something will work out." I sounded more confident than reasonable.

Ashely rubbed her shoulders as if her tension was increasing too. "What are you doing today? Do you think you can ask around about parking?"

"I planned to help Chris paint, at least one wall of the parlor, because he's getting a piano delivered on Monday."

"A piano? I didn't realize he played."

The thought of knowing something unique about Chris that Ashley didn't know surprised me. Not that it was a competition.

"He bought an antique piano at the estate sale, and yes, he's quite impressive."

"I appreciate your help setting him up for success."

"My pleasure." A slight twinge of remorse gnawed at me for keeping my feelings to myself.

Within the hour I pulled up in front of Chris's house.

He studied me and frowned. "Are you feeling well?" he asked with a protective tone.

"I have a headache but it's nothing. I'm tough." I shrugged the pain off, hoping to relieve the pressure behind my neck by rubbing it throughout the day.

"Stress maybe?"

I nodded. "Mountain life is more nerve-racking than living at the beach." I hit a sharp spot at the base of my neck, winced, and stopped massaging.

"It's not normally hectic here. What's going on?" he asked with his eyebrows furrowed, and the smile he wore when he first saw me fell from his face.

"Farmer John changed his mind about letting us use his field as the main source of event parking. Now what will we do?"

He winced. "This isn't your problem, Brittany. It's Joan's, since she's the boss and Ashley is off." The corners of his lips turned downward. "That's what vacation time is for."

"True, but I suspect Joan is trying to either fire Ashley or frustrate her to the point of quitting."

"No way. Why do something so ridiculous?"

I shook my head, perplexed.

"How about the abandoned store I showed you? The building is sitting there empty, so maybe the owner will allow the Candlelight Tour to use the parking lot. It's not as big as Farmer John's field, but it's a good alternative."

Appreciation overcame me. I stepped forward to hug him but then stopped. "Thank you. I'll let Ashley know." Our gazes met, lingered, and my escalating desire for him once again surprised me.

He must have recognized my change of vibe, stepping farther away and pointing to the supplies set out on the floor on a tarp.

"I don't mind cutting in since I have a steady hand," I suggested, referring to painting the area where the wall meets the floor or ceiling.

"Wonderful, and I prepped the walls last night." He ran a hand across the surface to make sure it was dry. "We'll just paint the wall where the piano goes. I can tackle the higher area if you want to paint lower."

I cocked my head toward him. "Thought you didn't have a steady hand?"

He smiled. "I'll just go slow and take my time. It's a patience problem more than anything."

"You seem patient to me, but okay." I carried the can outside to prevent paint from dripping on the hardwood floor by accident as I stirred. Prying the lid off the can took me a hot minute, but then I stirred until the warm-beige color mixed well. "This will look magnificent." Beige was a masculine color, perfect for an 1840s house and for Chris.

"A fresh coat will do wonders," he said, pouring the liquid into two disposable cups.

I hadn't pushed my luck today by playing music or turning on the tree lights. I thought perhaps he needed a break to adjust to the Christmas holiday in smaller increments. My efforts paid off, as he seemed more lighthearted, even whistling as he started to paint.

With two of us working diligently, the morning flew by. After we finished cutting in the paint, he rolled the wall while I decided to start by the fireplace since bookshelves took up most of the area.

Chris stopped painting mid-roll. "Why are you doing another wall? Thought we were just painting the one where the piano will go?"

The way he looked at me, with his eyes soft and gooey warm as though he'd known me a lifetime, made my belly flutter. Why was he staring at me like that?

"I need something to do. I can't stand here and watch while you work. "Besides, it's not like the painter will show up anytime soon." I held up the paintbrush playfully, a silly threat that I'd swipe him for questioning me. But I made sure to keep the brush over a drop cloth.

"Sassy today." He aimed the roller at me with a wide grin on his face. "Do you really want to challenge me while I have control of the roller?"

"No, I don't think I do." I giggled and got busy painting.

Before long we stopped to admire our handiwork. He stood close enough to me that his woodsy cologne made me yearn for him to hold me in his arms. No matter how hard I wanted to resist him, I found the chore difficult.

"You have a drop of paint on your cheek." He rubbed my face with his thumb, slowly and sensually. "Oops, I made it worse."

I didn't move, my gaze shifting to his inviting but serious eyes. His arms tightened around me in a hug, pulling me closer to him. The room faded and the blurry outline of Chris staring at me gave me the tingles. He leaned down, hesitated, and then pressed his lips on mine before he pulled back enough to assess if I minded the kiss. He had paint on his cheek, thanks to me.

I closed the gap between us, feeling his soft, commanding lips on mine. Then he deepened the kiss and I practically swooned. His strong arms around me kept me from sliding to the floor. We were made to fit into each other's arms. We kissed with desire, the sweetness overtaking me.

When he pulled back slightly, enough to take me in with his eyes, he smiled. "Are you okay?"

His warm breath danced on my face. "I don't know. Maybe try that again?"

A sound escaped his throat as he leaned in for a longer, deeper kiss. My insides tickled as though I rode a winding rollercoaster.

Ashley's ringtone on my cell jolted through my body. "Um, I need to answer," I whispered, not wanting to move away. He groaned and reluctantly released me. I dug the phone out of my back pocket, sighing to catch my breath. "Hello?" Chris and I might be standing ten feet apart, but my gaze never left his.

"You okay? You sound winded."

"I'm great." The familiar wave of guilt surfaced in me again but the thrill of his kiss delighted my heart.

"Can you come home? I need help making my lunch." She hesitated and asked, "Did I catch you at a bad time?" She sounded suspicious of my strange breathing and slow response.

"All is good." Trust me, life felt fantastic. "Let me clean up the painting mess and I'll be right there."

Chris watched me, his eyes wide with interest. When I hung up, he asked me with concern, "Is Ashley okay?"

I nodded, but my emotions were a mixed bag as he held my hand, his sexy gaze lingering on my mouth. A deep desire to kiss him again overcame me, but if I gave in to the temptation, I'd be late. I pulled away, hurrying to clean my paintbrush.

He helped, and when we finished and were at the front door, he pulled me into another long embrace, kissing me until I could barely catch my breath. There was something about this man that I found irresistible, intriguing, and unlike anyone I'd experienced before.

"We'll deal with that parking lot another day," he whispered, his mouth barely an inch from mine.

I swallowed hard to regain my composure. "Sounds good." I didn't want to leave his side, but duty called.

When I walked through the front door, Ashley was waiting in the kitchen. She had scattered a few lunch items across the countertop as though she had tried to make her own meal.

"I get frustrated by not being able to do something as simple as make a sandwich. I never realized how much I use my other arm." She sighed, glancing down at her sling.

"Sorry you're having to deal with this." Ashley looked so innocent, which sent another wave of guilt through me. Here I was, kissing the man she had a crush on, and he possibly had no idea.

How would he feel when he learned about her feelings toward him?

The Christmas tree lights in the living room blinked at him in mockery. A niggling sense of a long-forgotten memory nagged at Chris's mind.

The indistinct image of a woman resurfaced. She'd stopped by with a gift in her hands, and they were standing in the living room of his foster home. There was another woman present, the one who kept him, standing with her hand on his shoulder. He might have been five or six years old. The guest stepped in to hug him, but he didn't know her, didn't want the tight squeeze that followed.

The embrace felt familiar in a way that made him intuitively recognize her touch, but he never recalled meeting her before.

He startled and lost his connection, bringing him back to the present moment.

Focus harder.

Chris stared at the blinking tree lights in his living room, trying to concentrate so the image returned, maybe this time with more clarity. He brought her back into his consciousness, the room blurring into the lights of Christmas past. She cried, touching him as if he meant a lot to her, yet he didn't even know her name. No one made introductions, but she kept staring. When she handed him a gift, he resisted, not wanting anything from the odd stranger.

His foster mother instructed him to open the gift despite him wanting to hand it back. It took longer to open that present than any other, his confusion overwhelming. He'd never forget the emotions, but he wished he could remember her face. The box contained a brown diary and a pen with a feather. His foster mom told him to say thank you, and he obeyed, but he wondered what he was supposed to do with a notebook.

"It's to keep track of your thoughts," the woman said.

Years later, after keeping the diary in his sock drawer, he started writing his complicated views about his foster situation. He kept the diary with his socks still and hadn't read it in years.

Chris shook his head. He climbed the winding staircase upstairs with Bo following him and opened the top drawer to dig for the diary. Holding it in his hands now made him feel nostalgic.

He carried the diary downstairs and sat on the couch, staring at the worn brown leather diary, paging through, reading the musings of a hurt and confused child.

Bo scooted closer to him.

When he'd had enough, feeling heavy-minded now and lost in sad thoughts, he stood and turned off the tree lights. They represented a painful history, the very issues Brittany had suggested he let go of to move forward.

He didn't want Christmastime to remind him of his childhood, filled with sad memories. He was the man he'd become because of his experiences, and that man was good at business, even if he did shut out personal connections by working too much.

He suspected he needed to take a hard look at his early years and deal with unhealed pain. That sounded difficult, uncomfortable even, but it might offer him a better life.

As if Bo understood, he licked Chris on the cheek.

"I'm glad you're in my life, puppers. I didn't realize how lonely I was until you showed up." Bo whined and gave him another sloppy kiss. Chris laughed and wiped the wet streak off his cheek. Before now he wouldn't have appreciated a dog in his house or messy smooches.

The next afternoon, Chris took off work after the lunch rush to meet the delivery men. They transported the piano into the parlor and placed it against the newly painted wall, and the piano looked like it was meant for this exact spot and had always been there.

Brittany was right. It was past time to decorate his house and to live a fuller life, and he'd start by hosting Thanksgiving.

CHAPTER TWELVE

I rang the doorbell. Chris answered, looking casually dressed in a nice pair of jeans and a red long-sleeved shirt. His stiff posture made me think he was reluctant to open the door.

I held a covered casserole dish of stuffing I had paid a local caterer to make, and Ashley carried a bottle of wine. Two of Chris's employees, Susan and Tim, brought a dessert carrier and a paper bag of items with a long loaf of bread poking out of the top.

"Happy Friendsgiving," I said, instead of using the name Thanksgiving to give it more of a personal connection between all of us. I flashed Chris that smile I always wore whenever I saw him.

"You too. Come on in." He stepped back to invite us inside for the first dinner he'd apparently ever hosted in his house.

Bo barked, running in circles, Chris tried to keep him from jumping on his guests. The house filled with utter chaos. I walked toward the Christmas tree and turned on the lights as everyone except Chris strolled into the kitchen.

"Why don't you light these?" I asked, surprised. "They're always turned off."

He didn't answer at first, but when he did, his voice sounded deep. "I admit that the lights add to the festive ambience." Before I questioned him further, he turned on Christmas music. "Silent Night" floated through the house, and then Chris leaned down and wrapped me in a hug.

"It's good to see you." His warm breath tickled my face, making me snuggle into him more. Two days without visiting him seemed as though a week had passed.

"Thanks for inviting us over." I held onto him a little longer, hoping no one came looking for us. I was acutely aware of my surroundings to avoid Ashley seeing us.

"My pleasure." He planted a gentle kiss on my mouth. Keeping close, he said, "It's kind of nice having people I consider family in my home for the holiday. Let's go enjoy our guests, and I need to check on the turkey."

Ashley studied us as we entered the kitchen. Tim, the curly-haired server at Dog-Tired, opened a bottle of Sauvignon Blanc and began pouring the liquid into wine glasses.

Ashley sashayed up to Chris and placed her hand on his lower back. "The turkey smells amazing."

The way she grinned with blushed cheeks gave me pause. I watched as she guided him to the stove. Chris glanced back at me with a smile, giving me a wink. Then he stepped to the side to put more room between him and Ashley as he peeked into the oven.

"About forty minutes," he said to everyone. We were standing around the center island topped with snacks to hold us over until dinner.

I reached to make a small plate of vegetables with ranch dressing. Bo lingered as though waiting for me to drop something other than carrots or broccoli. "No begging, Bo."

He tilted his head, offering sweet puppy-dog eyes to make me feel guilty, but his tactics didn't work.

"How long will you be in town?" Susan asked me, dipping a miniature pretzel into a dab of dressing on her plate. She worked at Dog-Tired too, and I liked her friendly nature immediately.

"I love Snow Valley, but unfortunately I need to go home the day after Christmas." I glanced over at Chris and my cheeks warmed. Susan watched me with interest. "The people here are friendly," I continued, "and the town is precious enough to be right out of a romantic Christmas movie."

"What a great description of our town," Susan said, taking another bite of pretzel. A small piece broke off and fell onto the floor. Bo immediately devoured it. "Bo, you canine garbage disposal."

"Behave yourself, puppers," Chris said to Bo, although I knew firsthand that he fed the dog scraps. Chris opened the oven and maneuvered the pan of turkey onto the stovetop.

Ashley scooted closer to him. "Mmm smells divine." She leaned in and took a long whiff. "Need help cutting? I'm a pro."

Chris's eyes widened in humor and grinned lopsidedly. "Thanks, but that would be quite the trick with a sling. But don't worry, I can manhandle it once it cools off a little." He leaned away from her as if saying he wanted *her* to cool off too. "But would you mind setting the table?"

Ashley frowned but walked to the cabinet and began pulling out plates and silverware. I continued my conversation with Susan, who wanted to know more about my antique store.

Before long, Chris turned his attention to me. "Can you help me make the gravy?"

"I can do it," Ashley offered, stepping between us. I know she didn't mean to be rude on purpose, but she wanted Chris's attention.

He glanced around her and flashed me a sympathetic smile as if apologizing. Ashley frowned at me, and I felt the tension throughout my body.

"Chris, I noticed your piano in the parlor," Susan said. Her comment broke the tension and offered me relief. "I'd love to see it."

I sent Susan a silent thank you.

"Go ahead," I said to Chris. "Ashley and I will slice up the meat and make the gravy."

His face relaxed. "Thanks, and everything else is ready." They walked from the room chatting.

Ashley and I worked together in silence. I sliced the fragrant turkey, and she stirred the gravy. When we finished, I scooped the potatoes and gravy into decorative bowls and placed them on the counter next to a salad someone had brought. Tim helped me arrange everything, and Ashley called out that it was time to eat.

We sat around the table devouring our food, occasionally talking in between bites, just enjoying each other's company. Even Bo behaved by lying calmly on the floor next to Chris's feet, as if appreciating the friendship circle too.

"What do you usually do on Thanksgiving?" Susan asked me.

"I spend it with my family, but this year they're on a river cruise in Europe." I took a swallow of water to fight off a wave of nostalgia. "I miss them but hope they're having a blast."

"Oh, I've always wanted to take a river cruise, though I'm sure it's difficult for you not to have them home for the holidays. I'm glad we were able to get together," Susan said, pushing her plate to the side.

Chris smiled, visibly reveling in having his close friends gathered around him on the holiday. It beat staying home alone or working. Today showed growth on his part by allowing his home to be used for community and love.

Susan held up her wine glass. "To Chris, for hosting this fine meal and for adorning your house with the addition of beautiful antiques to get ready for the Candlelight Tour. Way to go! And happy Thanksgiving to everyone." We lifted our wine glasses and clinked them together. "We Wish You a Merry Christmas" played from the living room, filling me with joy.

His glance softened. "I can thank Brittany for the help. She has a special gift for picking out unique antiques and is a bargaining genius. I'm so glad all of you are here."

Everyone clapped, Ashley slapping her one hand against her leg. This was what supportive friends looked like. Chris had finally slowed down enough to enjoy their support.

"It's about time, Bro." Tim thumped Chris on the back. "Embracing the Christmas spirit is what it's all about."

Perhaps his thoughts about the holidays and inviting people to his house were changing.

After we finished eating, I helped rinse off and load the dishes into the dishwasher, resisting the temptation to reorganize them after

Chris placed several pots in precarious positions. Systematizing tasks was definitely my toxic trait.

"I can leave the rest until after everyone leaves," he said. Waiting to finish the dishes went against my natural grain too, but I promised to help him later. We moved out to the deck to enjoy the firepit. The sun had gone down, and white string lights added a comfortable feeling to the atmosphere. For someone who didn't like to entertain, Chris did an amazing job.

"What a fabulous view," I said in awe. The stunning violet hue of the tall ridge in the background blessed us with its beauty. The evening air smelled of evergreens and fresh mountain air. I could get used to this lifestyle, even if it didn't quite compare to the salty breeze of the ocean.

The black velvet sky and twinkling stars mesmerized me. The air became crisp despite the crackling fire. Chris sat next to me in an Adirondack chair, our knees touching. The warmth of his body made me want to snuggle closer, but I felt Ashley's stare through the flames. I despised this escalating strain between us, and we'd need to have another one of our girl talks. I still believed in our core promise to each other to never let a man come between us.

We had to fix this issue. She was my beloved cousin, a best friend, a person who I cherished. I came to Snow Valley to help her however she needed, not to ruin our relationship.

I vowed then and there, no matter how Chris made me feel, that I would prioritize Ashley's feelings.

Thanksgiving dinner turned out better than Chris expected. If someone had asked him a year ago to host a holiday for friends at his house, he would have turned them down as fast as they asked. But Brittany challenged him to move forward and he had accepted.

He wasn't sure why he agreed, except Brittany brought out a loving, vulnerable side of him he never knew existed. What a stroke of genius to encourage him to join the Candlelight Tour and to push him outside his comfort zone. Decorating his house made it feel more like a home. With her presence in his life, he felt the rough exterior wall he'd built beginning to crumble. She was unique, full of life and innocence. When he was around her, he felt lighter, freer, and … happy.

But Ashley was becoming almost possessive over him. Where had that come from? They had never been a couple or dated, yet she behaved as though they were together when she helped him prepare the Thanksgiving meal.

She almost seemed to intentionally ignore Brittany.

While he never wanted to come between them, he was not interested in Ashley romantically. He never noticed her interest in him before, but tonight she had made her desires known. He couldn't have been the only one to notice.

After everyone left, he got comfortable on the couch and stared at the Christmas tree. The lights twinkled in the dark room, mesmerizing him. As if in a meditative state, a memory overcame him. He sat silently in his own thoughts.

The memory was of the same woman. He was older in the vision but still couldn't remember her in vivid detail. He saw her bouncy, shoulder-length brown hair, and she walked hunched, as if the weight of her troubles pressed down on her shoulders.

She didn't hand him a gift but offered a hug instead. "You will always be a part of my life, even if I don't know you well. I can't attend your school activities and am limited to visiting you every few years, but just know I love you."

Her words confused him, but he had nodded. A strange thought overcame him. He remembered thinking she was a distant relative, a cousin maybe, but now he knew for sure she was his mother. If he'd known that then! He'd never met a man in his life who popped in and out like she had, only the woman.

The next revelation shook him. He'd seen her sitting in the bleachers waving to him when he graduated high school. He had thrown his cap into the air, and then spotted her, letting the cap land at his feet. His friend stood next to him and asked who she was, but Chris shrugged.

It was sad that she no longer came around now that he had become an adult. How convenient. He'd have numerous questions for her, and maybe that was why she stayed away. Unless something happened to her over the years. Another sad thought.

Chris let the thoughts of her drift away as he watched the blinking lights. He usually overworked at the restaurant, keeping busy to avoid his thoughts, yet this year, here he was, ironically staring at the lights. Talk about being triggered. His heart ached.

Brittany's presence went a long way in filling some portion of that gaping hole in his life. He didn't want her to leave and return to the beach, but she would. No matter how hard he tried to keep his distance from her emotionally to protect himself, his attraction had taken on a life of its own.

He was falling in love with her.

CHAPTER THIRTEEN

Chris's text this morning concerned me.

I debated telling Ashley about this new dilemma but the task of helping her finish a shower and getting dressed had completely worn her out.

When my phone beeped again, I had no choice. I held the screen up for her to see.

"What's that?" She leaned in closer to read his words. "Are you kidding?"

"Nope." I rubbed my face to release tension. "How will we get his house ready in time for the Candlelight Tour if he can't take off any more work to help? The painters can't come until right before the event, if they show up at all."

"I don't know. What else needs to be done?"

"At least one piece of furniture we bought at the estate sale needs refinishing, although Chris promised us a week of dinners at Dog-Tired if I do the work." I chewed on my lower lip. "The floors need a healthy dose of polish, the walls need painting, and we need more Christmas decorations, like greenery." I inhaled a long breath and found irony in the fact that I experienced more stress visiting Ashley than running my own business at home.

"It's my problem more than yours. Sorry, Cuz." Ashley's face fell into a frown, her forehead crinkled with worry lines. "I didn't mean to dump the Candlelight Tour on you."

"I promised that I'd help you, and we are in this together." Although that wasn't completely true. She was physically incapacitated. Without Chris's house in the Candlelight Tour,

Ashley would likely be fired. I imagined terminating her bordered on illegal, or at the very least unethical, but they'd find a way once she returned since this was a right to-work-state. That meant an employer had the right to fire someone without providing a reason.

Ashley reached forward with her good arm to grab a blueberry muffin off a plate on the far side of the counter and winced.

I pushed the plate closer to her. "Does your arm hurt more today?"

"Yes, even if I wiggle my toes, but it's time to take pain medication." She shoved a bite of muffin into her mouth, washing it down with orange juice and a pill.

Poor girl. How awful having your life limited to a medication schedule so you felt decent enough to do half your normal routine. I bet it was even difficult to hold a book with one hand and try to turn the pages. Thankfully, she was making progress.

"What are you planning to do today?" she asked, flashing me a pointed look that made me feel guilty.

"Well, I had planned to help Chris refurbish the antique table." It was the one that held the porcelain figurines of a man and woman. "Without his help, hanging out at his house feels awkward."

Ashley sighed. Was her reaction out of relief that I wouldn't be spending time with him or frustration that his home wasn't near ready?

"I understand he needs to work," I said, defending him.

"Me too, but you shouldn't have to restore his house and furniture without his assistance." Ashley pushed the empty plate aside. "Helping him is a dilemma."

"How so?"

"I don't think it's fair that you should fix up his place without him, but he's a workaholic and leaving work is a challenge. I mean, I want his home on the Candlelight Tour but at what cost? It's too much to ask of you both."

"What will you do if you lose your job?"

Ashley glanced out the window. "I don't know." She turned her attention back on me. "Maybe he'll pay you to do the work?"

"It's awkward to charge him to prepare his house for an event he doesn't want to participate in to begin with." I stood, collected the plates, and brought them to the sink to rinse before I set them in the dishwasher, which I rearranged to keep from going batty.

"True, but you *are* improving his living space."

"A space he was fine living in before I came along to change everything." I suspected he didn't like modifications to his simple life, based on his hesitation to adopt Bo. He'd had an unstable childhood and probably liked controlling his environment to provide consistency for himself.

In all truth, I didn't like changes myself. I believed that reaching beyond the safety of a person's comfort zone provided an opportunity for growth, but here I was, living in the same small town where I grew up. Perhaps I held my own desires for control over my life. Didn't we all to some extent?

After I had Ashley settled for the day, I picked up my keys.

Ashley raised her eyebrows and gave me a questioning look. "Where are you headed?"

She knew exactly where I was going. "To Chris's. I can't let your company fire you for something I can help with." Plus, I didn't mind refinishing his gorgeous table.

Chris had left the piece of furniture in his garage behind his house. He'd placed it on a tarp and left a space heater in case I got cold. What surprised me was that he also left a note, thanking me. He also mentioned he'd bring me lunch after the rush. And a thermos of hot chocolate awaited me.

Warmth swirled inside me, making me feel adored and yummy.

On the surface Chris seemed to keep people at a safe distance, but I sensed he had a sensitive side and a lot of affection to give to someone he trusted.

Bo curled into a blanket while I worked up a light sweat sanding the table. I hoped to keep the original color but it was in worse shape than I had first thought. I jumped when Chris called my name from behind.

"Sorry," he said, watching me with a gentle smile on his face. He held a to-go bag in his hand and shook it to tempt me.

"Guess I was concentrating." I wiped my hands on a rag and he closed the distance, each step increasing the chemistry between us. I needed to prioritize Ashley's feelings. Remember?

His smile turned to a grin as he watched me.

Warmth circulated through my body, causing my cheeks to burn. But that didn't stop me from stepping into his open arms. Despite the bag he held, he wrapped his arms around me, holding me tight, and he pressed his lips into mine. I felt his desire for me all the way to my toes.

He deepened our kiss, the warmth of his mouth inviting.

I melted into his arms, feeling lightheaded and overtaken with emotion. It was easy to imagine being with this man the rest of my life.

Ashley. Remember her.

When he pulled away, I caught a draft and shivered.

"Cold?" He wrapped a relaxed arm around my shoulders, our bodies fitting together nicely, and guided me to the table to admire my work. "Wow, you know your stuff. I'm impressed."

"Flattery will get you almost anything." I dragged in a long, calming breath to try to reduce my excitement.

"Almost?" His eyes flashed humor mixed with longing, yet restraint.

My belly swirled as though I rode a steep and fast rollercoaster. "If you keep looking at me like that, we'll miss lunch."

He laughed, his gaze never leaving mine. "Promise?"

My cheeks burned hotter. Thankfully, he ended the flirtation by rattling the to-go bag. "Okay, I'll behave. Let's eat lunch in the kitchen where it's warm."

Bo got up, stretched, and then sniffed the bag. Chris rubbed behind the dog's ears, his expression toward me turning soft and full of admiration.

"I'm surprised you left Bo home. It's my turn to be impressed," I remarked, happy to see Chris's growing connection with Bo.

"The temps dropped overnight. When I opened the door to leave for work, he wanted to stay behind, so I let him. I didn't feel right about making him fend for himself in the cold." He rubbed his hand down Bo's back, and the dog moved closer to lean against Chris's leg. "Well, let's eat lunch."

He led the way to the back door of his home and opened the kitchen door for us.

The warmth of his house engulfed me. Not that it was exactly cold in the garage because of the space heater, but the house felt more welcoming. While Chris pulled out the contents of the bag and put it on the table, I retrieved plates and silverware. We sat close to each other while Bo watched us from his nearby dog bed. I practically inhaled the food.

"You must have worked up an appetite." He grinned at me as I took a large bite of the best chicken sandwich I'd ever tasted.

I chewed, nudging him with my elbow.

"Ouch, that's a sharp bone you have there." He rubbed his arm in complaint.

We laughed together, and I had to cover my mouth to keep the contents from falling out.

His expression grew serious. "This is a lot of fun. You're an attractive, irresistible best friend."

I managed to swallow, promising myself to take smaller bites. After a big gulp of water to wash down the food, I said, "You are too. And it's refreshing."

He leaned in closer but didn't kiss me. "I like you much more than just a friend."

My mouth parched, and I suddenly needed another drink of water but didn't move. I sat there like a goofy schoolgirl, crushing on the cutest boy in the class. But he was more than a boy. He was the sexiest man I'd ever met. And by sexy I didn't mean just in looks, but in mannerisms, intellect, his kind way of treating me.

We sat there with our lips less than an inch away. Goosebumps rose on my arms, making me shiver. Somewhere along the way my heart became invested, and I refused to figure out how I'd deal with my feelings when it came time for me to leave. I'd embrace the present moment, completely unlike my usual need for planning.

Chris gave me a quick kiss and pulled back to finish eating. After a bite or two, he said, "Let's go snow tubing."

"Huh?"

"Don't tell me you've never been snow tubing." He chuckled, obviously thinking my lack of snow experience was funny.

"I've been tubing behind a boat. Does that count?" Some of my favorite memories happened when my family owned a boat. "We spent many weekends hopping to different dredging islands in the intracoastal waterway. My favorite one is Bear Island and has sugar white sand with water so green you'd think you were in the Caribbean."

"Such a different lifestyle than here." His facial expression turned somber for a flash as he ate the last of the sandwich.

"But I'd love to try snow." I was up for adventurous activities, especially when it involved spending more time with him.

"Great, I look forward to it." He stood, cleaned up the paper wrappers, and tossed them into the trash can. "Make sure to dress in layers, a non-cotton shirt as the bottom choice so the material won't retain sweat. It'll help to keep you dry. Then layer from there, ending with your coat, a stocking hat, and waterproof gloves. Also, wear waterproof boots or shoes designed to repel water."

"Aye aye, Captain." I saluted, feeling comfortable around him.

"You're talking boat talk." He laughed. You can take the woman from the beach but will never take the beach out of the woman."

Neither of us moved, avoiding looking at each other. The truth hit a little too close to home.

CHAPTER FOURTEEN

I woke up several times throughout the night, and too early in the morning. Before the sun rose, I had my shower out of the way and breakfast on the table. Eventually, Ashley stumbled into the kitchen, rubbing the sleep out of her eyes.

"Good morning," I sang to her, and then to the Christmas music playing in the background.

"Aren't we Susie Sunshine." Her voice sounded grumpy. "But I hope you enjoy tubing today. You'll love it." Her voice fell flat, as though she struggled to wish me a fun day.

"If you prefer that I stay home …"

"No, go enjoy your day!" She made an effort to inject enthusiasm into her tone.

"I'm so confused, Ashley. I've been wanting to talk to you." I took a long breath in, held it, and then let it out. "I don't know how to put what I'm feeling into words."

She looked me square in the eyes. "I know what you're going to say.

I turned my head, looking at the time on the microwave clock. Chris was going to be here soon.

"I know you and Chris care about each other, and I'm trying to deal with my emotions, but I understand you need to be happy too." She reached out and touched my elbow. "But I'll be honest. I'm struggling."

"Understandable." I glanced up at the ceiling and sighed. "I never want anyone to come in between our relationship."

"Me, either," she said. "There's no easy answer here."

I heard Chris's truck pull into the driveway.

"Go. We'll figure it out later." Ashley got up and left the room.

Being a pleaser by nature, my habit included prioritizing everyone else before myself. My trip to the mountains was teaching me to let go of other people's expectations and to live my life. Besides, who knew when I'd get another opportunity to tube down a mountain. Even though I had agreed to travel here to help Ashley, I didn't need to feel guilty for taking a few hours off.

And even if I didn't know all the answers, I had a right to be happy. Ashley had a choice too. She could either accept my feelings for Chris or let him come between us.

I pulled on my thick winter coat and gear and hurried outside, practically bumping into him.

"Someone's excited to go tubing." He bent over to give me a bulky half-hug.

Goosebumps ran up my arms, and a strong sense overcame me that Ashley was watching us through the window. While I didn't want to hurt anyone deliberately, I also had to convince myself that I wasn't doing anything wrong.

He took my gloved hand as we walked down the icy steps to the truck. "You look well outfitted for a cold day sliding down a hill."

"Hope so. It's a lot chillier up here than at the beach, but I can handle it. I kept waking up last night, excited about today." I hadn't been transparent with a man in a long while and now was as good a time as any. I found him easy to talk to.

"Me too. I couldn't sleep, either." He reached across the seat and held my hand as we drove on curvy roads toward our adventure. We passed by a scenic overpass that took my breath away. A blanket of haze layered the base of the valley today and the colors of the trees muted. Chris steered around a windy dip in the road, pavement wet and covered by smoky fog that hovered in the low spots. The occasional icy spots added a winter feeling to the day.

The man sitting next to me seemed content, just as happy to spend time with me as I was with him.

He reached over to the radio and turned on Christmas music. The lyrics to "Santa Claus is Coming to Town" filled the truck.

"You've got to be kidding? *You* turned on holiday music?"

He flashed a grin at me. "Well, of course. My lady loves the jolly ole songs."

My lady …

The music set the tone for the day. Once we arrived, Chris bought us tickets. We had an hour wait before it was our turn. Christmas music played, wired outside, and we stood near the fire pit. We chatted about Dog-Tired, Bo, and what needed finishing to prepare his house on time, which made my belly anxious. I tried not to let the topic ruin my lighthearted mood.

Chris glanced at his watch. "You ready?"

"Yes!"

We rode a magic carpet escalator up the hill as the excitement swirled through me. At the top, I marveled at how the fog seemed even thicker in the valley and along the snowy edge of the forest from this vantage point. The trees held no snow on their branches. We maneuvered our way to the tubes and climbing in was awkward with all my layers of winter clothes. I gave Chris a flirty grin as he waited on the icy run next to mine. I was already having fun.

A young man dressed in coveralls instructed me to hold on and to keep my feet up. He gave me a shove, and off I went. As the speed increased, I screeched. The cold breeze made my cheeks hurt. Bumping along at a surprisingly fast pace, my tube zipped down the hill and I held on tighter. This must be what it was like to fly.

I hit the snowbank with a jolt, and my tube spun around to travel backward. Not being able to see where I was headed gave the illusion of travelling faster and my belly flipped. I started laughing. What fun!

I twisted around and caught sight of Chris's back. Not that I was competitive, but I wanted to win the unspoken race between us, though there was no chance of catching up to him. My tube made a scraping sound when it ran across the rough surface at the bottom of the hill, where he now stood waiting for me.

"What do you think?" His white teeth glistened against the backdrop of snow.

"At first I had concerns, especially when I spun around to finish the hill backward." I hadn't experienced this sense of joy with a man before. "But I loved it! Let's go down again."

He grinned even bigger and wrapped his arm around me. "That's my girl!"

There was *my girl* again. I didn't allow myself to overthink what his words might mean. We stepped onto the magic carpet for another go. He snuggled in close against my backside, his arms wrapped around me.

The next zip down the run, I knew what to expect. Chilly air on my face, cold tight cheeks … My smile from laughing seemed to freeze in time. I enjoyed the bouncing of the tube, including the airborne moments that made me feel like I was a weightless astronaut in outer space. Like playful kids on a holiday break, we repeatedly rode the magic carpet up the mountain and then sailed down at fast speeds.

The sun burned off the fog, and the neon blue sky added to our glorious mood.

Before the last trip down the hill, I grabbed hold of a large snowball. When we reached the bottom, I pelted it at him, hitting him in the arm of his coat with a splat. Without pausing, he tossed one back at me. We laughed like teenagers who had a crush on each other. Then he scooped me into his arms and gave me a toe-curling, delicious kiss.

"Want some hot chocolate?" he asked, taking my gloved hand.

"Sounds great." Although I was already warm with all the layers I wore. I removed my coat, knit hat, and gloves while he ordered our drinks. He was such a gentleman, considerate, and fun as well. With the paper cups in hand, he nodded toward a picnic table not too far from the firepit.

"Here you go." He passed me a cup and we sat down.

"I've never had so much fun," I said, then blew on my melting whipped cream.

"Really? I bet you have fun water skiing."

I nodded, a handful of childhood memories resurfacing in my mind. "True, but we don't have our boat anymore. To be honest, I work all the time."

He attempted to take a sip but it was apparently too hot, so he blew into the cup. "Sounds like me."

"The two of us have no life outside of work, though I used to think I did." I managed to take a small sip and instantly regretted my mistake when the hot liquid burned my tongue.

"Let's make a pact while you are here." He placed his hot chocolate on the table, and I followed suit to give it time to cool. "I think we should enjoy life together as much as possible. It's good for both of us."

I chuckled, feeling years younger at the thought of playing. "Love the idea. What do you have in mind?"

"Hmmmm. For starters, have you ever taken a winter mountain hike?"

I shook my head. "Of course not."

"We need to change that up. We can hike to a frozen waterfall, but let's wait until the next snowfall so the woods look like a winter wonderland." He picked up his cup, blew on the thin layer of now melted cream, and took a drink. "Perfect temperature."

"The hot chocolate or the winter hike?" I laughed playfully, leaning into him. Never had I felt so much like myself around a man.

"Both, but I meant the hot chocolate." He leaned down and gave me a gentle kiss.

His lips tasted like chocolate dipped in vanilla ice cream. After he leaned back to take another sip, I sampled mine. "Mmm, perfect." The crisp air had cooled our drinks off. Then a thought popped into my mind. "Question. I thought you couldn't leave the restaurant to work on the house, so how can you escape to play now?"

"Busted. I don't enjoy handiwork. I'm not made for painting and refurbishing furniture. I'd much rather manage Dog-Tired." He swiveled around on the bench and leaned back against the picnic table, one arm around me and the other holding his almost empty cup.

"I appreciate your honesty, but Ashley is counting on us." I glanced into his gentle eyes. "No offense but your house still needs a lot of work before the Candlelight Tour. It will come faster than either of us think."

My father always kept our house in tip-top shape. I didn't understand how Chris could ignore projects. It was difficult to imagine living with someone who didn't prioritize the cleanliness and upkeep of his home.

"Are you Ms. Neat and Tidy?" he asked, a hint of concern in his voice.

I shrugged, but since he had admitted the truth to me, I said, "Guilty. I'm off on Sundays and Mondays from the store, so I clean on Sundays. That way I can enjoy a clutter-free house the rest of what I call my weekend."

He flinched. "I don't have a cleaning schedule, and the chore gets done whenever I think about it or if someone is coming to visit."

"No wonder being part of the Candlelight Tour concerns you, but the house needs to be in good shape cosmetically. Cleaning is a given." I studied him as he shifted his attention to two teenagers holding hands and approaching the bonfire. Was he distracted or ignoring the topic of discussion?

"Chris?" I waited for him to look at me. "Promise me everything will be ready for that important event. Ashley's job depends on the success of the Candlelight Tour."

"What do you mean? I thought she was using vacation days?"

"She is, but she has a new boss who scrutinizes everything, even though she's technically off work." I rolled my eyes before turning to study the cute young couple snuggled into each other near the fire pit.

"They can't hold her responsible for the Candlelight Tour then." We watched the couple, who were now kissing like we had been earlier.

My heart did a little squeeze. They were adorable, and I realized we were too. "Right or wrong, that's the situation and why I'm helping her."

"I did wonder why you were involved in the Candlelight Tour when I thought you came up here to help her in general. Are they paying you to fill in?" When I shook my head, he added, "That's not right. You are a sweetheart for helping Ashley."

"No big deal, but I want to see her keep her job. Instead of hiking, although that sounds wonderful, let's put the same effort into preparing your house." Being organized and planning details characterized who I was as a person. I suspected Chris's principles were different than mine, at least when it came to caring for his home. The old saying that opposites attract didn't seem so outlandish.

Not that I planned to marry him.

The fact we lived almost three hundred miles apart never left my mind for long.

He groaned. "Let's mix it up a bit. I'll commit to taking off afternoons. We can alternate the days by playing, which I think is just as much of a priority as the house, and the other days to complete household projects. Deal?"

I shook my head and nudged him when his mouth dropped open. "Let's tweak the priorities a bit. We play one day for every four days we work on the Candlelight Tour."

He remained silent too long but then shrugged. "You're a task master. How about for every two days of work."

"No way. And I inherited the task master gene from my parents."

"Are you ever impulsive?"

I had to think about his question. "Nope, don't think I am. Except I drove up to help Ashley, if that counts."

"Not really. You knew ahead of time and planned how to pull off the trip." He crunched his cup in his hand, standing up and taking mine to throw away. "I have a challenge for you."

I sat still.

He laughed at my hesitance and offered me his hand to encourage me to stand. "Fair is fair, my lady. Since you need help being more spontaneous, I'll come up with the activities we'll do on our playful dates."

Dates. And he kept tossing romantic pet names at me, like my girl, or my lady. Did he think we were dating? Maybe we were technically, since he had paid for snow tubing and the hot chocolate, but I saw us as just having fun together.

Oh, come on. I mean, we kiss each other.

He led the way back to the truck, my ungloved hand tingling at his touch. When we reached his vehicle, he bent down to give me a soft kiss before opening the passenger side of the truck.

And I'm falling in love with him.

CHAPTER FIFTEEN

The next afternoon I met Ashley's coworkers at Dog-Tired to discuss the progress of the Candlelight Tour. Ashely only had a few days left before she went back to work, so she joined us in the discussion.

We sat at a far corner table next to the window. Light snowflakes blew outside, dancing in the air like little ballerinas before dotting the window and melting as soon as they hit the glass. Susan, the sweet woman I met at Friendsgiving, delivered a round of water along with iced tea or mugs of hot chocolate.

Her face lit up when she saw me. "Hi, Brittany. Good to see you again."

"You too. We have to start meeting like this more often." I marveled at the positive vibes she gave off both times we met. She reminded me a bit of my mother, comforting and friendly, and made me miss her. I hoped they were having fun on their vacation.

"Anytime. If you need any help readying Chris's house for the Candlelight Tour, I'd love to assist. I'm known for my decorating skills, especially for the holidays. I can also bake and have an eye for setting up appetizer trays."

The others watched me closely, listening to the conversation. They probably wondered how I knew Susan and what my involvement was with decorating Chris's house and managing food preparation for the Candlelight Tour. I didn't want them to know the personal details.

Susan took our order, jotting notes on a worn notepad. When it came my turn, I ordered a French dip sandwich with Swiss cheese and a side of homemade Au Jus, along with a salad to replace the French fries for my daily dose of veggies. Once everyone finished ordering, the meeting began.

Lynda, wearing a soft cream-colored angora sweater, turned to Ashley and me. "You're doing a wonderful job. We have a full list of houses, and Chris's home is a pleasant surprise."

I smiled but let Ashley accept the praise. She deferred the compliment by nodding at me. I didn't accept the recognition and tapped her on the unaffected arm. "Even though Ashley is on vacation, she has still been a trooper."

Joan, the epitome of a stoic boss, stared at me without smiling. I didn't care if she knew I was helping or not. I wasn't about to allow her to devalue Ashley.

"How is the menu going? Do we have a list of who is serving what at their house?" Virginia, her long brown hair in a loose braid, opened her notebook, pen ready.

I remained silent so Ashley had to answer. Next week she'd be dealing with the project on her own part time, at least as far as the team knew. Until the actual Candlelight Tour ended, though, I'd be assisting however she needed me to make the event beyond successful.

Ashley thumbed a few pages in her notebook and tapped the top of the page with her ink pen. She read off the menu list, stopping when she came to Chris. "He's serving squares of homemade desserts that will knock everyone's socks off."

"I didn't know he could bake," Lynda commented.

He wasn't making the items himself, but they didn't need to know the particulars. He just needed to hold up his end of the deal by keeping his home in the Candlelight Tour and providing food.

"He owns a restaurant, so of course he can bake," Ashley said in a pleasant voice. Because I'd known her all my life, I knew she was biting back a tart comment to defend him.

"Will his house be ready?" Joan asked, contorting her face in disbelief.

"Of course," Ashley said without hesitance. "He's been working on it daily."

All three women stared at us. True, Chris had earned the label of workaholic at Dog-Tired, not of taking care of Amelia House, but he was trying.

"I'd like to help with decorations," Virginia said with a soft voice. "It's my favorite part, and I know Chris doesn't enjoy the holiday festivities." She pointed at the sparse multi-colored lights strewn along the edge of the ceiling in his restaurant. Nothing else adorned the dining room to celebrate Christmas cheer. "He needs a Christmas tree in here."

Before Ashley turned down the offer, I interjected. "We could use all the help possible. Thanks."

Ashley glared at me as if I'd invited the enemy to assist us. With less than three weeks left until the event, fixing up Chris's house remained the goal and required a team effort. I'd learned a long time ago that it was best to work together with your coworkers. Even though Joan had a chip on her shoulder, the other two ladies wanted to help Ashley.

Kat served us our food and Chris joined to say hello to everyone. Our gazes met and held, catching the attention of the others. No one said anything, but I knew they were curious. I turned away from his gentle eyes and saw Ashley cross her arms. While I held empathy for her, the parameters of their friendship had nothing to do with me.

I silently applauded not feeling the need to please everyone all the time. Yes, I deserved love too. Refusing to sacrifice my own happiness to please other people was exhilarating. Mentally I patted myself on the back. Of course, this change didn't mean I didn't care about people, because I did. I loved Ashley like a sister.

Susan stopped by to check on us, focusing her attention on me. Admiration sparkled in her kind eyes. I figured she appreciated my devotion to helping Chris. "Is the food above everyone's standards?"

"Absolutely," I answered for the group because I'd listened to the raving comments throughout the meal.

She grinned, clearing a few plates before leaving us to our conversation about decorating Chris's house.

"Let's set a date." Virginia pulled out a small planner from her purse. "How about this Wednesday, let's say one o'clock."

I chewed on my lower lip, calculating how long the floor project might take before we embarked on decorating.

Joan took my hesitance as resistance. She turned her attention to Ashley. "Unless you prefer to handle the project yourself next week after you return to work." She eyed Ashley's sling. "If you can handle the job."

Ashley didn't react, but instead responded in a calm, professional voice. "A team effort is always appreciated."

I wanted to chuckle at how Ashley's words implied that this endeavor had not been a team effort from day one.

"If anyone wants to help move furniture tonight and to clean the floors so we can start polishing tomorrow, then Wednesday might work." They stared at me.

"You're polishing floors?" Joan asked.

I made eye contact with Joan and leaned forward to make myself clear. "Yes."

"I'll help," Virginia said, glancing at her coworker as if encouraging her to offer.

"I'm willing," Lynda said with some hesitance in her voice. "That's too much for one or two people. And I agree, the floors need to look fresh."

I smiled. The team mindset had shifted.

Ashley dabbed the corners of her eyes with a napkin. "Thanks, y'all. I appreciate everyone stepping forward to volunteer. I'll be there to at least give support."

"Wonderful. Chris and I can move the furniture, Virginia and Lynda can start washing the floors with a gentle cleaner, and Ashley can supervise." I never saw myself as a manager, having been a one-person operation at Time-Worn Treasures with occasional assistance.

Yet another skill the mountains had taught me.

Chris approached our table again, and we agreed to meet at his house after work.

"What condition are the floors in and what is involved?" Lynda asked.

Chris glanced around the table, sighing with relief. "Thank you. A few years ago, I had the floors restored professionally. While I haven't done much to keep them conditioned, I'd say they need a light cleaning and polishing to make them shine."

I spoke up. "I've been researching what steps are involved, and basically, we use a wood-floor cleaner to remove dirt and grime before we can apply polish that's specifically designed for old wood floors. I also consulted with a preservation expert to make sure my knowledge is accurate."

Chris winked at me, and the others watched us with interest.

He said, "The restoration begins tonight at my house."

Chris and I worked together to remove the furniture from his living room. We placed washcloths underneath the legs of the settee to avoid scratching the floor.

"On the count of three, push," I said to him. "One, two, three." We slid the heavy love seat across the floor and maneuvered it into the kitchen and against the far wall. The doorbell chimed.

"Got it!" Ashley made her way to the front door. The hallway filled with women's voices, and then I heard Ashley take charge by assigning them tasks.

Ashley dust mopped one-handed while Lynda began at the opposite side of the room, and Virginia trailed behind with a mop, using the gentle cleaner I had chosen.

"Make sure you use minimal water," I suggested to allow for faster drying times as well as protection of the wood. The overhead fan helped speed up the process. We worked together, and Ashley practically glowed with gratitude. My admiration grew for these women working together to reach our goal.

"And to get into the spirit of why we are doing all this, let's play Christmas music," Ashley said, and Virginia clapped.

But Lynda and Chris groaned.

"Oh, come on," I said. "You're on the committee for the Candlelight Tour, Lynda, so let's embrace the festivities. The tasks will be more fun that way." I realized not everyone enjoyed the holiday, depending on their own personal experiences and beliefs, but we were throwing a Christmas event. The music fit the scene.

"Brittany, help me place these washcloths under the legs of the stand to move the Christmas tree into the parlor." Chris kneeled beside the tree, waiting for me to help him.

"Crazy that you have to move a decorated tree." Lynda studied the situation. "I can't imagine that will go well."

"No worries." Chris placed the folded washcloth underneath the stand as I steadied the trunk. His confidence and positive tone lent us assurance. Sure enough, we scooted the tree into the parlor without losing an ornament.

"Next job." Chris lifted the end of the long couch, and I placed a washcloth underneath each leg so we could safely move the piece of furniture across the floor. When it came time to scoot the couch into the kitchen, I struggled to push my side, even with washcloths underneath, so Lynda joined me. Teamwork!

The kitchen filled up fast as we moved furniture in. The last item was the coffee table. We had to squeeze it in between the stove and the love seat.

Chris whistled. "That barely fit."

Lynda returned to the living room to mop, and I sat on the arm of the settee in the kitchen to rest for a moment. Chris stepped closer to me, his thigh touching my knee. He leaned down and gently pressed his lips against mine. They felt warm and enticing, but I worried about someone walking in and catching us kissing. He didn't move away, and before long I no longer cared who saw us.

A shuffling noise caught my attention as someone bumped into a stack of boxes filled with books. I glanced up to witness Ashley standing there, bright-eyed, mouth dropped open. She hurried from the room, knocking the top box off the stack with a crash.

Chris kissed me once more and then pulled away. "Guess our secret is no longer between us. Are you okay?" His tone held trepidation, although it was a risk we had both taken.

"Guess it was a matter of time. I think she suspected all along." I hated that for Ashley.

Chris gave me a peck near the corner of my mouth and then tapped my knee as he pulled away to clean up the mess of books on the floor.

I decided to let my cousin process what she saw instead of pulling her aside to talk. Chris's house wasn't the right place to have an in-depth discussion.

I didn't look forward to the conversation with Ashley that awaited me tonight, but her pain was my discomfort. I'd hurt her feelings with Chris.

When we returned to the living room to assess progress, I noticed Ashley studying the fireplace.

"The mantel needs a coat of paint, and so do the walls. When is the painter coming?" She didn't make eye contact with me, directing the question to Chris.

"That's the problem," Chris answered. "He continues to say he's showing up in a few days or a week but never does. I explained the urgency of the situation with the home tour, but the project he's working on currently is taking longer than he anticipated."

Ashley sighed, shaking her head. "What are we going to do? The tour is in nineteen days."

"I don't know. I'm not a painter, and I can't keep missing all this work." Chris ran his hand through his hair. "Can't we light the room with candles instead? No one will be able to see the walls."

"Great idea but not ideal," I said, inserting myself into the conversation. "Safety first, besides people need to see each other to engage in conversation. They also paid for tickets to admire the historic houses."

Ashley nodded, turning away from me.

Why did relationships have to be so difficult? I always thought cousin love would conquer all, and we had promised each other years ago to never let a man come between us. Up until now, we had different dating types and never went after the same person, so it had never been problematic.

But here we were.

Suddenly I felt selfish because Chris was a vacation romance, someone to enjoy life with while I stayed in town. But if I were being honest with myself, I'd have to admit my heart might be involved.

My shop waited for me, along with the familiarity of a town I loved. My parents still lived in the home I grew up in. Security and safety remained important to me.

Suddenly I realized what I had done. By pouring myself into the home tour, I had temporarily filled a hole in my life because this was the first year my family hadn't gathered for my favorite holiday of the year. Here I was, living through Ashley's friends to fulfill me, and I had just hurt her to the point she refused to talk or look at me.

But Chris was different, unlike anyone I'd ever met. When I spent time with him my spirit lifted. It was like breathing in the fresh scent of the ocean after a summer storm.

What a dilemma.

"We're going to have to paint the walls ourselves," Ashley said, her words intruding on my complicated thoughts.

"I'm done with the restoration. It's too much to ask when I'm needed at work and you have one available arm." Chris glanced at me. "And she's here to help you with your care, not to paint my house."

"I don't mind," I said. "When you love someone, you do what's required to make it through rough times."

CHAPTER SIXTEEN

The following afternoon the four of us met again to polish the floor. Already, with just a good cleaning, the natural shine glistened with rich hues. I loved restoration projects and considered them a way to bring the past into the present.

I tested an inconspicuous spot on the floor to make sure the polish didn't damage the wood. Smiling, I said, "Look at that."

Chris whistled. "I've never seen my floors look so nice."

My smile turned into a wide grin. "That's my plan. I want to wow everyone who steps foot in this house." I glanced up at him, happy to see his face glowing with excitement.

"You know your work, Cuz." Ashley beamed with pride and patted me on the back.

"I can't take credit. The floors are naturally beautiful." Deep inside, though, I was glad they appreciated how the hardwoods looked so far.

It surprised me that Ashley spoke to me today. Last night had grown too late for a conversation, and we'd gone to bed exhausted without addressing what had happened with Chris and the kiss. I'd admit, Ashley had always called me the queen of avoiding conflict, and she was right. My lack of conflict resolution usually blew up and bit me with a vengeance. But it was hard to change a toxic habit.

We each worked a manageable section and applied the polish with soft, microfiber mops. Ashley headed toward the kitchen to make us a snack of cheese, crackers, and a plate of fruit to keep our energy level elevated.

Fresh, cold mountain air filtered in through the open windows for ventilation, and the scent of pines made the Christmas season come to life. A snippet of warm sun lit up the living room as beams of light flooded through the side windows near the fireplace and highlighted the floor.

I watched as everyone worked hard. "Make sure you go with the wood grain, and only apply a small portion of polish," I reminded. Heads nodded.

After we finished applying the first coat, we stopped long enough to eat snacks, waiting in the parlor until Ashley called us into the kitchen.

I studied the hardwoods in the room and frowned. "I thought the parlor floor didn't need polishing, but after seeing the results in the living room, I'm changing my mind."

Chris let out a long sigh. "Time is not our friend. There's no way we will accomplish everything on your to-do list." He stared at me.

I stared back. "But I want the downstairs to look spectacular." The event wasn't even my baby, so why did I take such pride in sprucing up the place? What was I trying to prove to myself or others?

"Brittany, the house doesn't have to be perfect." His gaze didn't waver from mine. "It's one evening for a couple of hours."

"I admit, I have perfectionistic tendencies. But what do I let go?" I frowned in frustration.

"Painting the walls and refinishing the floor in the parlor." He crossed his arms.

My lower lip jutted out.

"I'm drawing the line here. No to the paint and the parlor hardwoods. We've done enough and I'm over it."

"Don't you want to make a statement?"

He shook his head. "I don't care what other people think. Besides, my restaurant is my baby, not my parlor."

I couldn't relate. I viewed my home as my neat and tidy peaceful place.

"Enough is enough." He remained grounded, not budging.

The others watched us in silence.

"What can I say? It's your house, but can we at least paint the walls in the living room?"

"Nope. After this project, I'm finished. And don't forget we're supposed to play too, not just work." His face remained tight, and I realized we just had our first disagreement.

I shifted my weight, not answering.

"I think you need a good reminder about a healthy work-play balance." He watched me closely, remaining firm, but his tone held a gentle touch.

"You're one to talk," Ashley said. "I think you both need to learn to play more." She hurried from the room.

Neither Chris nor I moved. We weren't in competition, and the decision was his. *Let it go.*

I moved forward but so did he, and we bumped into each other.

"We're not on the same page today." He frowned at me, and I shrugged. He was right.

"I understand your point," I said, releasing the desire to be right. "But I don't do anything halfway." Like he said, it was his house, not mine.

He took my hand and pulled me close. Our lips met, his mouth warm and practically melting me into a puddle like the sun thawing a frozen bank of snow.

Ashley cleared her throat. "Come on, love birds." She must have come back to see why we hadn't followed the rest of the group into the kitchen.

After our snack, we finished the floors in a couple of hours. The hardwoods looked amazing and we left tired and happy. All I wanted was to mentally check out and watch a movie once we returned home. But no such luck. Ashely pounced on me like a mountain lion attacking prey.

"When are you going to learn to address issues as they happen?" she asked, waving her hands around.

I sat in stunned silence.

"Remember how we made a pact to never let a man come between us?" Ashley frowned, and I shifted in my chair.

Talk to her! Stop avoiding tough conversations.

"I do remember, and honestly, I had no intentions to get involved with Chris." There, I acknowledged the issue. Sort of.

She glared at me.

"Ashley, I would never do anything to intentionally hurt you, but I can't help fate. We were drawn together to help each other."

"Help each other how?"

"He has issues stepping outside his comfort zone and so do I." Chris thought of Ashley as a friend, but it wasn't my place to tell her, and I suspected she now understood. "We both have issues dealing with past relationships, overworking, and learning to enjoy life."

"I suppose you want me to think you are the perfect match for each other. What happens when you leave?"

I shrugged, not wanting to think about the day I drove out of town without him. "I don't have the details figured out yet. Going home is inevitable, and neither of us want a long-distance relationship."

She sighed and collapsed on the couch. "You're going to hurt him."

"That's not my plan." But she was right. "When I leave town, we'll both feel miserable."

Ashley wiped her eyes with the back of her hand. "I assumed you knew I had feelings for him."

Her words struck me like a sharp knife. This was why I despised conflict. Nothing good seemed to come out of facing problems.

"I'm sorry, Cuz." I climbed from my chair and wrapped her in a hug. "You're the last person on Earth that I want to hurt." When my phone rang, I jumped. "Ashley, I need to answer this because Nancy never calls me unless it's an emergency."

"Work as always." Ashley left the room, leaving me to decide between hurrying after her or answering the call.

Relationships were complicated.

The fact that I had to choose didn't sit right with me. My shop was important, but so was Ashley.

I chose to answer on the last ring, before voicemail kicked in. "What's up?" Maybe if I answered casually, any issues with Nancy and Time-Worn Treasures would go away.

Nancy knew me well. "The store is fine, but I have a problem." She paused, and I knew the news wasn't good.

"What's happening?" My pulse rate sped up. I went into my bedroom and closed the door behind me for privacy and then sat down on my bed.

"It's my father. He had a stroke and is in the ICU at Mercy Hospital." She began to sniffle. "I'm packing my bag to stay with my mother, and it's a four-hour drive. I realize how important it is that I run your shop, but my mom isn't sure Dad's going to recover. The hospital staff encouraged family to be there."

"I'm so sorry." My heart sank at the thought of what Nancy and her family were experiencing. "Of course you need to be with your dad."

"I hate to disappoint you but I closed the store. It's up to you whether you return or not, but I can put a sign on the door if you want."

"We're closed tomorrow anyway, so I'll leave in the morning to drive back." I rubbed the back of my neck to relieve the headache beginning to form. "Please be careful driving, and I hope your dad is okay. Let your mom know I'm sending all of you healing thoughts."

"I appreciate it, and again, I'm sorry to bail on you."

"Family comes first, always." When we hung up, my own words stung me. Ashley was family, and I had to leave her to fend for herself right before the Candlelight Tour. As I mentioned to Chris, I didn't do anything halfway, yet here I was, planning to leave in the morning. At least Ashley was feeling better, but Chris needed me too. He'd agreed to the Candlelight Tour because I asked him with the promise I'd help. I had done a lot, but not enough.

I strolled into the kitchen and found Ashley eating leftover turkey and stuffing from our Friendsgiving.

When Ashley saw me, she set her fork down with a clank. "What's wrong?"

"Your intuition amazes me." I explained to her what happened and how I planned to leave first thing in the morning.

The tension we'd experienced moments before visibly dissipated. "We'll be fine. I'm sorry for earlier. Your store is important, and you need to be there." She stood and wrapped an arm around me. "I appreciate everything you've done here, and I'm doing much better, thanks to you."

I smiled but it was an act more than anything. My emotions circled all over the place. "Oh! I'm supposed to hike tomorrow with Chris."

"Trust me, he'll get over it."

I pouted, not liking her answer. "What about the Candlelight Tour?"

She shook her head. "He'll be fine. I'll make sure he is."

A slight smile crossed her face. She must have realized because in a flash her expression turned serious. Maybe she was happy I was leaving so I wasn't competition for her with Chris?

No, Ashley wasn't like that. At some point I had to leave for home. This was just a bit sooner than planned.

"I'll tell Chris what happened. He'll understand." Again, the corners of her mouth held the slightest upturn as though hiding back a smile.

Talk to her. Address the awkward moment.

"Despite what it seems, I'm not trying to come between your friendship with Chris." I tried my best to soften the words.

She shook her head too fast. "Not at all. We will always remain friends."

"Good, your friendship is important." What I left out was how Ashley seemed to like him more than friends, but it wasn't my business. Not really.

"That's right." Her voice held a slight edge.

I had one last chance before I left to try to address the kiss between Chris and me, and my confusion about their friendship. "When I first arrived, I thought you were trying to fix me up with Chris, but when you saw us kiss, I got the vibes that you were upset."

She shrugged. "Nah, it was just a kiss. It didn't mean anything."

But it did mean something, more than I let on even to myself.

"He knows you were leaving after Christmas, so maybe he's practicing."

I sighed, dissatisfied with how the conversation was going. "Practicing for what?"

"Jumping back into dating." Her face lit up as though he might date her now.

I rubbed my face to relieve tension. "Ashley, he sees you as a sister." Oops, I hadn't meant to let the secret out.

Her jaw dropped but she recovered quickly, too quickly. "I'll let him know what happened and that you had to leave." She gave me a hug and then pushed me away.

"Thanks, but I'll give him a call." I walked back to my room, once again closing the door. I sat on my bed and dialed his number but the call went to voicemail. I hung up, but then called back to leave a message but somehow his voicemail was now full. I texted him, instead, explaining the situation briefly, telling him about Nancy's father and that I couldn't hike tomorrow because I needed to drive home. I apologized and promised to keep in touch.

He hadn't replied by the following morning, so I texted once more to wish him the best of luck with the Candlelight Tour, and how I'd be thinking about him. Still no response. I drove by his house, but his truck wasn't there, so I drove by the restaurant.

"He's not here," Susan said. "He took the day off but sorry to see you leave so soon." She gave me a hug, once again reminding me how much she resembled my own mother.

"I will miss all of you." I glanced around Dog-Tired, taking it all in. "I'll miss this place too."

"It's hard to believe the time has come for you to leave, but you have a life at the beach." She squeezed my hand. "Come visit us soon."

I nodded, knowing how difficult it would be to leave my store once business picked up after the holidays. I regretted that my last interaction with Chris ended over his house project and how he was done with the restoration.

The one time I faced my fear of conflict, it ignited like paper on embers in a fireplace. Not once, but twice—Ashley and Chris—in the same day.

The drive home was long and silent. No phone calls, no texts, no Chris.

CHAPTER SEVENTEEN

Chris paced back and forth across the pristine hardwood floor in the living room as Ashley dashed about, setting out plates for the Candlelight Tour. Every nook and cranny of his home reminded him of Brittany, from the hardwood floors to the Christmas tree, even the kitchen, because of Friendsgiving.

He hadn't realized how much he'd fallen for Brittany.

"A dollar for your thoughts?" Ashley asked.

"Wow, inflation. It used to be a penny." Chris forced a smile but laughing was out of the question.

She closed the distance between them and wrapped him in a half-hug. Resisting the urge to retreat, but not wanting to give her the wrong idea, he stiffened. There was nothing wrong with Ashley. She was great, but he only wanted to date Brittany. Unfortunately, she wasn't here for the big evening they had worked so hard to achieve.

"Don't skate around the issue, my friend. I know you care for Brittany, and the feeling is mutual. I know I've had a lot of my own feelings to figure out, but I realize you two are meant to be together. If you need someone to talk to, feel free." She gave him a squeeze and pulled away.

He glanced at her. "You're right. Guess I just wished Brittany were here. We all worked so hard to prepare for this event, and now she's at the beach."

"We'll make it enjoyable." She glanced around the house. "The place looks wonderful, and the living room floors shine. You can't tell the walls didn't get painted or the parlor floors weren't refinished, and the house looks elegant."

"Thanks." Brittany would have noticed those items hadn't been done, but no one else seemed to care. The battery-operated candles flickered shadows on the walls, and Christmas music lent a festive ambience to the event. He couldn't stop thinking about Brittany. Losing her reminded him of all the loss he'd had, especially over the holidays. Maybe liking Christmas just wasn't meant to be for him.

"Call her," Ashley urged.

He shrugged and avoided her gaze. "It hurts too much."

Someone tapped on the door and a small group of visitors entered and milled around the room. An older woman named Elizabeth gasped, placing her hand over her mouth. "Look at this place! I feel as if I stepped back into time when the house was in its glory." She and her husband, William, shook hands with Chris and made introductions. He'd known of them but had never met them, as they ran in higher circles than he ever had. "I've always wanted to see your home, but it had never been on the Candlelight Tour before."

"Thank you. This is the first year." He didn't explain that he never cared about the tour and that he'd only agreed because of Brittany.

Virginia approached them with a tray of small desserts. "There is more on the table. Help yourself to anything you'd like to sample." She held out the tray to Elizabeth and William.

Elizabeth's face lit up. "Don't mind if I do." She helped herself to a small slice of pound cake with a swipe of preserves on top and took a bite. "Mmm, delicious. I'd love to have the recipe."

"You can ask our dear friend, Dottie," Virginia said. "All of her jams and breads are delicious."

"I'd say. I should have known Dottie made this. I love her banana nut bread and her shop. I frequent the store often." She dabbed at the corner of her mouth with a napkin. "Anyway, good choice to have her cater," she said to Chris.

"Glad you're enjoying the pound cake." Virginia gave a pleasant smile and turned to offer another guest a sampling.

Elizabeth turned her attention back to Chris. "Maybe they'll restore the abandoned carpet store to its magnificent historical presence, just like your home." She leaned in closer. "We parked there tonight, and what a great choice. There was plenty of room." She lowered her voice. "I've heard they've been working on a big remodel the past couple of days, although the windows were still boarded and I couldn't see a thing."

"The news makes my evening even better. I'm glad they're doing something with the building." Chris loved the old storefront and wished they would restore all the houses and shops on Main Street, as long as it wasn't him doing the restoration. He'd had enough to last him two lifetimes. "What business is going in there?"

"A small grocery store, from what I hear. We could use another option." She clucked her tongue, apparently unhappy about having only one choice in their small town. "Especially if they offer fresh deli sandwiches and specialty items."

"That would be nice, but Dog-Tired has a good selection of deli sandwiches for lunch. I'll give you a ten percent discount on your first visit." He'd never seen her and William in the restaurant before, and he was always looking for opportunities to attract new patrons.

"That's very kind of you. We'll make sure to take you up on your offer." Elizabeth caught the elbow of someone she knew, and her husband followed.

He studied them from afar, missing Brittany even more.

The Christmas tree glittered. The holiday music tugged at his heartstrings.

As soon as everyone left, he leaned back into the couch and studied the tree. The Christmas music still played, but it sounded louder now that the guests had left. The successful evening made him proud of all the hard work they had achieved, a task that had seemed far-fetched a month ago.

The Christmas tree stirred up old feelings of loneliness and inadequacy. He stood and yanked the plug from the wall. The holiday music seemed to grow louder, blotting out whatever cheer he'd felt earlier tonight. One click on his phone ended the annoying tunes.

He removed an ornament from the tree, and then another, unable to bear the artificial cheer of the lights blinking at him in mockery.

Stop. Leave the tree alone.

He planned to spend Christmas Day with Ashley, Susan, Kat, and Tim. The thought of Brittany's absence tasted like bitter cranberry sauce that was missing a healthy dose of sweetener.

Call her.

No.

He wanted more than a mere phone conversation.

My store welcomed me with the old familiar smell of antiques. An older lady I'd never seen before huddled in the back corner, lifting an antique lamp to study the price tag. Otherwise, the shop was quiet two days before Christmas Eve. Stock was low even though I had added my purchases from Snow Valley, including the beloved broach I'd love to keep for myself. It was worth too much money not to sell.

The holiday music tried to cheer me up but to no avail. In fact, the joyful songs caused me to miss Snow Valley, Ashley and her friends, but most of all Chris. I picked up the cell phone to check messages but there were none. Several times I wanted to call him, but my pride kept me from dialing his number. He never responded to my voicemails, and his lack of care hurt me. I thought we were closer than that.

I shrugged off my thoughts because they made no sense. I lived here and he resided in Snow Valley. The inevitable pain I tried to avoid by getting involved with him snuck up on me and clocked me over the head. How had I allowed my feelings to get involved?

The phone rang and I answered. "Nancy, how's your dad?"

She sighed into the phone. "It's been intense, and we thought he was going to make it, but he didn't. I didn't have the energy to call you to tell you he died the evening I drove up here. The funeral arrangements are tomorrow." A long swish of breath sounded into the earpiece. "We wanted to have everything finished before the holidays, so I plan to be home on Christmas Eve."

A lump formed in my throat. "I'm so sorry to hear about your dad. I know how close you were." The sentiment sounded ridiculous to my own ears, but it was all I knew to say.

"Thank you." Silence filled the space between us for an awkward moment. "How was Snow Valley? Such a beautiful place this time of year. Anytime, actually."

That was a complicated question. "It was wonderful, and I learned a lot about myself."

"How so?"

"I learned to stop putting my needs last, even if it hurts the feelings of people you love."

"Oh, no! Did that happen?" Nancy's voice perked up. At least my problems offered her a possible distraction from her father.

"Pretty much." I filled her in on what happened with Chris, giving her a short synopsis instead of boring her with details.

Nancy let out a long sigh. "Sounds rough. How did he handle you coming back home?"

It was my turn to sigh. "Not well. I'm pretty sure he'll never forgive me for abandoning him right before the Candlelight Tour, and when I called him twice, he didn't return my messages." Reliving the thought made me shiver.

"Are you okay?" My customer, the elderly woman I'd seen earlier, stood at the counter with the lamp she had been scrutinizing for so long. I had forgotten she was in the shop.

I jumped. "No, no. I'm fine. Sorry about that," I said to the lady.

"Are you talking to me?" Nancy's voice reverberated in my ear, and I hurried to end the call to tend to my customer. I rang up the purchase, the high sale amount barely penetrating my heavy mood. "Would you like this protected in tissue paper and gift wrapped?"

"That sounds fine. It will save me from having to wrap it last minute." The broach displayed on the counter caught her attention. "Beautiful!" She fingered the expensive piece and glanced at the price tag. "I'll have to come back to get this."

My heart sank but I tried to pull off a fake smile. "I found it at an estate sale in the mountains, and I love it too." I had discovered that patrons loved to hear about how I stumbled on the pieces I bought, as well as any known history, and personalizing the items usually led to a sale.

"I need to do my research before I purchase such a treasured piece. I'm thinking of buying it for my own Christmas present."

I folded tissue paper and placed it in a box around the lamp for protection. "What a great idea, buying yourself a gift." I should have kept the broach for my Christmas gift to myself since I'd be celebrating the holidays at home alone, but now the woman was interested. I wrapped the package, fighting off a wave of nostalgia. Family memories of opening presents with my parents at their house and then eating homemade lasagna wandered through my mind.

But now, the day would be quiet, and I didn't even have a Christmas tree.

"You look sad," the woman commented.

"I'm sorry. Guess I'm missing old family traditions this year." I shook off my thoughts and forced another fake smile. "My family is out of the country so this year will be different." I had no idea why I was sharing my thoughts with a stranger.

She tilted her head and touched my hand with hers. "I have a feeling your holiday will be just fine. Do something nice for yourself."

A little smile escaped the corner of my mouth. "Thanks. I'll do just that." I think I had a small pre-lit tree in the attic and could dust off the branches and plug it in. I'd play some holiday music, buy a store-bought lasagna, and make the best of the day. And in the meantime, I'd try not to think of Chris and the friends' holiday I had been looking forward to.

CHAPTER EIGHTEEN

Thick snowflakes melted on Chris's windshield almost as fast as they landed. Wipers swished back and forth on full throttle, drowning out the faint holiday music playing in his truck. He didn't know what had gotten in to him to listen to the festive songs, but the tunes lifted his mood each mile he traveled. Bo laid in the backseat, already napping.

Christmas Eve had arrived in no time, and he wasn't about to participate in the festivities without Brittany. She was the epitome of holiday spirit. Each mile he drove to the beach, the slower the snow fell, the faster his heartbeat pounded at the thought of seeing her again.

She didn't know he was making the drive, and he hoped she'd forgive him for not returning her calls. The thought of losing her hurt too dang much. Ashley had encouraged him to call, but instead, he decided to make the trip to spend the holidays with Brittany, knowing she was alone without family.

The morning was young. He'd woken up before the sun rose and headed off to coastal North Carolina. Ashley had given him Brittany's address as well as the shop's. He had five hours and ten minutes left. He hadn't been on the road long, but snow slowed him down even more.

He found himself humming to the music and had even turned up the tunes once without realizing. Brittany had a hold on his heart that refused to let go. Otherwise, he wouldn't be taking a road trip on a snowy morning so they could spend Christmas Eve and day together. If that wasn't love, then he had no idea the definition of the word.

Hours went by in slow motion but at least the snow had stopped falling. As he entered the small town of Seaview—what a name!—he slowed to absorb the festive atmosphere. Lit-up decorative seashells and anchors placed on black ornate lampposts lined the streets. A large Christmas tree perched in the town's square, adorned by the biggest ornaments he'd ever seen. He swore he had just landed in a Christmas movie, minus the snow.

Patrons in lightweight coats perused the streets to finish last-minute holiday shopping. A bar and grill, similar to Dog-Tired, caught his attention. He fought off the urge to stop and check out the place, wanting to find Brittany, to hold her in his arms, as soon as possible. Two women left a bookstore with bags in their hands, and a gentleman walked the sidewalk carrying a paper cup of coffee.

What a charming place, and he could see why she loved it here. In some ways it reminded him of Snow Valley, minus the snow.

He did a doubletake as he passed by a quaint store on the corner named Time-Worn Treasures. A sign out front marked the shop as open, so he parallel parked his truck. Thankfully, the street parking was almost deserted, otherwise he would have had difficulty squeezing in between two cars. Neither of the vehicles looked like hers, but maybe she parked in the alley.

When he stepped out of the truck, a wave of warmth hit him square in the face. The temperature had to be almost forty degrees warmer. Amazing how such a difference was possible with just three hundred miles between them.

Bo sat up and whined.

"It's okay, boy. Stay here and I'll be back in a few."

Bo let out a whimper of protest but laid back down.

Chris headed toward the shop, feeling her presence. The big bay window held a fuzzy blanket, an old rocker with a book placed on the seat, and an antique night table with a vintage lamp. Brittany knew how to decorate to create a welcoming ambience. He'd heard compliments time after time from visitors on the Candlelight Tour, and he agreed. She had done a magnificent job bringing life to his house and recreating a feel of history.

As he entered, a bell chimed. An older woman stood behind the counter, and disappointment filled him. Perhaps Brittany was in the back room.

"Welcome to Time-Worn Treasures. Is there anything in particular you're looking for?"

He wanted to speak up, to ask for Brittany, but a familiar broach diverted his attention. It was the one Brittany found at the auction.

"That's a beauty of a piece," the woman said. "It's received a lot of interest, and one woman said she was coming back for it, but in the meantime, it waits to bless someone on Christmas morning." The employee misunderstood his intentions for being in the shop.

"I'm looking for Brittany. I'm a friend of hers."

The lady gave him a good once over. "She's not here right now."

He frowned, the disappointment almost unbearable. "Is she at home?"

To his surprise, she shook her head. "No, she left town."

"Left town," he repeated as though he hadn't heard her correctly.

The woman grinned. "She went to the mountains to visit family, and a special friend." She cocked her head to the side and raised her eyebrows.

Chris smiled, giving her a nod. "Guess I better be heading back to the mountains if I want to make it before dark."

"Good idea." Her smile grew bigger, and he knew Brittany had mentioned him to her.

The drive back was slower than the ride down, and this time he was driving in full-blown snow. It pelted against the window, the wipers streaking the slushy mess back and forth. The truck's headlights were met with fog, and the curvy roads were barely passable. He tried to imagine Brittany sitting in front of a cozy warm fire at Ashley's place, and he regretted not asking the woman at the shop how long ago that Brittany had left.

Please, oh please, let Brittany be safe.

He misjudged the turn by going too fast. His truck slid off the side of the road and hit a snowbank.

I strained to see out the windshield as I clenched the steering wheel with a death grip. Nothing but white covered my field of vision as I slowly made my way down the mountain road. Certainly, Snow Valley had to be around this turn.

I'd been driving for close to seven hours instead of the usual five and a half. No one was on the road, which meant no one was going to save me if I slid into a ditch. I thought back to the slippery night Chris pulled my car out. He had no idea I was here, driving in this storm. It didn't help that my cell phone had no service, which was the norm on the backroads of the Smokey Mountains.

Christmas music kept me sane with its upbeat lyrics and jingle bells. Too bad Santa and his reindeer weren't real because I could use some help. It was Christmas Eve, and the last place I wanted to spend the holiday was in a car alone on a dark, foggy mountain road. But Chris was worth the effort, and I needed him in my life.

Had I made a wrong turn? A blanket of snow covered the highway signs, as well as the roads.

My palms sweated from my grip on the steering wheel. *Come on, keep going.* The road had to lead to a town, or to a house, eventually. I had to be close to Snow Valley, right?

Headlights behind me lit up my dark car like a floodlight. The beam felt oddly calming. The thought of sharing the road with someone on this long stretch was comforting, but it also made visibility challenging.

The falling snow streaked my windshield and partially obscured my view.

I didn't see the snowy ice patch until too late. My car slid to the right side of the road, and I gasped. There was no guardrail, and the drop off was likely steep, cloaked by a black abyss that haunted me. But a daunting tree stood in my path. I steered to the left, but my car didn't respond. Right before I nearly crashed into the tree, my car grazed a snowbank, and I yelped. My car jolted and then slid to the left into the oncoming lane, toward a steep rock base.

"Get your act together!" I commanded myself. *Straighten the car slowly, no fast movements.* Turning the wheel, I was able to straddle the center of the road. Thankfully, as I rounded the bend, no other cars were coming toward me. Other people had more sense than to travel in this weather except for the vehicle keeping its distance behind me.

Breathe. One. Two. Three.

Up ahead I saw a twinkling light off in the inky distance. Right now, I'd take a house to stop at, maybe knock on the stranger's door, and beg for mercy or a phone. Who would I call? Chris?

He'd be the only one willing to take a chance on driving to pick me up on a night like this.

Another light twinkled in the night. And then another. A town up ahead, and I prayed it was Snow Valley.

I relaxed my grip slightly, the song on the radio drawing my attention. *Good tidings we bring you and your kin. We wish you a merry Christmas and a happy new year.*

Snow Valley felt like I was coming home to family and friends.

The truck followed me into town, and to my surprise the vehicle turned onto Ashley's street and pulled into her driveway behind me.

I parked, my body trembling.

Someone pulled open my door and leaned in to wrap his arms around me.

He pressed his warm lips against mine, making me melt into him. I looked up into his eyes, shadowed by the lamp near the sidewalk. "Chris," I managed to say.

"Oh, sweetheart." He locked his mouth on mine, kissing me like I've never been kissed before. He pulled away slowly. "You almost went off the cliff, and I held my breath. I didn't know it was you at first but figured whoever you were, you weren't used to driving in such bad weather. I felt for you, knowing you were someone's wife or girlfriend, and wondered how a man could let his beloved drive in the awful weather. Then I recognized the make and model of your car, and the license plate."

"My license plate?"

He tilted his head back and gave a tight laugh. "I realize it's an odd habit. It comes from the fear of people leaving me. I reasoned if I remembered their license plate, I'd be able to track them down if they left me."

"Oh, Chris!" I held him tight. "I don't want to ever leave you again."

He looked at me with surprise. "What are you saying?"

"I'm staying here and buying the old, abandoned store. I'll make it into an antique shop and live in the above apartment."

A strange gurgling noise sounded from his throat. "While that sounds great, someone bought the store. They're going to put a specialty grocery store in the building."

I gawked at him in the light of the outdoor lamp, not understanding what he was saying. "That can't be. I bought the place and know nothing about a grocery store."

"You bought the place?"

I nodded. "Yes, the deal is done. I signed the paperwork."

He picked me up and twirled me in a circle as the snowflakes landed on my cheeks. "You're staying, as in moving here?"

"Yes, I'm going to expand Time-Worn Treasures to Snow Valley. I'll have to go home at least once a month to train Nancy and to restock the store with antiques. Snow Valley needs an antique store. There are so many estate sales here, and this place is chock full of historic antiques."

He laughed like a madman into the night. Snow fell around us, causing my hair to stick to my face and my cheeks to turn cold. But I didn't care. I was with the man I loved.

"Does Ashley know?"

"She does, but I made her pinky swear over the phone that she wouldn't tell you." My voice was an octave higher than usual, and I giggled. "I wanted to let you know myself."

"She didn't whisper a word." He took my hand as we headed up Ashley's walkway but a howl stopped us in our tracks.

"Hold on a minute." Chris picked his way back to his truck and opened the door. A flash of black hopped from the seat.

Bo greeted me with a bark, whines, and when I bent down, he showered me with wet dog kisses. "Oh, Bo! I missed you too, buddy." I squeezed him tight, not wanting to let go.

Chris laughed and took my gloved hand. We walked toward Ashley's house while Bo jogged ahead of us.

I stopped and tugged on Chris's hand. "How was the Candlelight Tour?"

"It went without a hitch, but it was sad without you. I missed you something fierce, but the house received a lot of compliments, and several people commented on the beautiful living room floors. And not one person mentioned the walls not being painted." He tapped me on the butt and laughed. "I have to say it: I told you so."

Oh, how I loved this man. I wrapped my arms around him, snuggling into him. "They were probably being polite because no one could miss the unpainted walls, but glad the night went well. I knew you could do it with Ashley's help."

He bent down, kissing me on the tip of my nose. "Amelia House also won the Historical Preservation Award."

"What?" I pulled away enough to see the falling snow and his face in the glow of the lamp. "Congratulations!"

"I couldn't have done it without you." He bent down but paused, his mouth so close to mine. "Brittany, I love you," he whispered.

I held my breath, knowing he wouldn't say those words to just anyone. When I was able to speak, I said, "I love you too."

He took my hands. "I want to live forever with you. We've just met, but I already know you are the person for me."

Was he proposing?

"This isn't the right place, but will you marry me, Brittany my love?" His voice quivered, and he held my hands. "If you say yes, I will buy you a ring and propose right, but until then, I want to know we are on the same page."

My mind spun in circles, and I felt warm all over despite the cold, falling snow. I couldn't stop grinning. "I'll hold off on answering you until we make it official, but I can say we share the same reason as to why I'm moving here. I don't want to live without you."

He gave me a long, tender kiss that made my belly spin.

"Kids, are you coming inside or are you going to stand outside in the cold all night, making out like schoolkids?" Ashley's voice rang out in the night, piercing the quiet.

"Give us a minute." He pulled me into his arms and held me against his chest.

I felt his muscular arms through his puffy winter coat and knew I was safe, in the protective arms of a man who loved me.

"I will love you forever." He cupped my faced and our warm lips met once more.

Forever sounded surreal and wonderful. And despite my parents being gone for Christmas, tonight turned out well. I knew I needed to have a long discussion with Ashley, and not avoid the conversation like I usually did.

I needed her blessing.

CHAPTER NINETEEN

The following morning, I woke up to blaring Christmas music and the aroma of coffee and pancakes. I closed my eyes again to process all the changes in my life. Great changes, even if my parents were in another country celebrating their own Christmas without me.

Good for them!

I reflected on how much I'd grown from the woman-child who was upset that she wasn't going to spend the holidays with them. Remembering that awkward conversation, I now found it selfish. I was a grown woman, and my parents had a right to pursue their dreams of traveling on a cruise.

In pursuit of their vision, I had found my own, ones I didn't even realize I held. Not only had I traveled to the mountains to help my cousin when she was in a desperate place in her life, but I met the man of my dreams, and I expanded my antique business as well as relocating to Snow Valley.

What changes I had made in less than two months!

Today I was spending Christmas lunch and the rest of the evening with new friends, Ashley, and Chris. I also planned to have a long talk with Ashley this morning and face my fear of conflict. It was time to stop hiding from difficult conversations, time to grow up and welcome the woman I had become.

I wanted Ashley to accept that Chris was the love of my life, but if she didn't, I wasn't sure how I planned to move forward. I wouldn't give up the relationship of a lifetime, but I also wanted to honor my agreement with Ashley to always safeguard our special relationship.

What a tough predicament but one I no longer wanted to hide from.

I crawled from bed, my heart racing. The hot steaming water of my shower felt wonderful on my aching shoulders, thanks to my death-hold on the steering wheel last night. Perhaps I was procrastinating by showering too long, and I reminded myself I was no longer that woman.

I was strong, capable of buying a building to expand my business without discussing it with anyone except Ashley. I had driven in a wicked snowstorm to be with the man I love and that was a big deal.

I'm a boss girl and own my power.

Then get down there and have an adult conversation with my cousin.

I dressed in a hurry, deciding that I wasn't nervous but excited. I read somewhere that those two emotions came from the same place, but one was fear-based and the other joy-based.

When I entered the kitchen, my belly growled. "Mmm smells delicious. What a way to wake up." Delightful Christmas tunes flooded the room.

Ashley laughed. "It's my turn to take care of you." Then she started to sing. "*I'm dreaming of a white Christmas. Just like the ones I used to know. Where the treetops glisten ...*"

I smiled to myself and stared out the window at my first white Christmas. The sun reflected off puffs of white covering the bushes, the trees, the sidewalk. What a glorious morning.

"Have a seat at the countertop." Ashley placed a plate of blueberry pancakes and bacon in front of me, along with a cup of juice. It was her turn to cook me breakfast, and I was proud of the progress with her arm.

"You know how to make a holiday morning special." I watched as Ashley made her own plate and sat down beside me. We ate in silence while I contemplated how to bring up the topic of Chris.

When we finished, I pushed my plate aside. "I want your blessing for something important to me."

"Of course, I always support you," Ashley said, grinning. "I'm glad you're here."

"And I'm glad to be back. I do have a request, and it's a big one." Here it goes, no more hiding behind the fear of confronting the topic of Chris and me. At her nod, I continued. "As you probably realize, Chris and I have some unexpected feelings toward each other. I tried to avoid the situation because I suspected you have strong feelings for him, and we agreed to never let anyone come between us."

She remained silent.

I fidgeted in my seat but kept going. "We didn't realize until after I left how we felt about each other. I'd like to know your thoughts."

Her face grew tight, and her demeanor turned rigid. I wasn't good at reading someone's thoughts, but hers were obvious.

I braced myself for an argument, but I had to be honest with her. "I didn't set out to fall for him and hope you can forgive me. I'm moving here so Chris and I can be together."

Her mouth dropped open. "I can't lie, my heart hurts a little that he didn't choose me. But I love you and want you to be happy. You are both good people and deserve each other. I love you." Tears slid down her face and she held me tight. "I know you'll treat him right."

I hugged her hard, tears falling from my eyes, but the relationship we'd found in each other as adults was priceless.

Ashley and I drove separately to the Christmas festivities at Chris's house. I wanted to arrive early to help him bake lasagna and to set up for our party, and Ashley had a few last-minute presents to wrap for our gift exchange. Thankfully, I had already bought gifts for everyone.

Chris and Bo answered the door, chaos ensuing from barks and dog dances. Chris swept me into a robust hug and then gave me a delicious kiss.

"You're playing Christmas music," I exclaimed, surprised.

"You are a good influence on me. After you left Snow Valley, I almost took the Christmas tree down, but I left it up because when it was lit, you were close by."

"I believe that is the sweetest thing anyone has ever said to me." I slipped into his arms, and he bent down to give me a sweet kiss.

"I'm so glad you're here. I have something for you." He pulled away, taking me by the hand and leading me into the living room. "I hope you like it."

I took a small box with red ribbon from him, thinking it could have easily been a ring box except it was wrapped, and he wasn't down on one knee. I glanced up at him. "You don't want to wait until the gift exchange?"

"No, this is special and deserves a private moment." He stood nearby like a boy excited to open his own box on Christmas morning, except my name was scrawled in slanted writing on the tag. "Go ahead, open it."

I found his huge grin endearing. "Okay, but you have to wait until later for yours." I took my time untying the ribbon and unwrapping each side of the taped silver paper.

Bo nosed me and sniffed the package.

"Hurry up, already," Chris complained, so I went slower just to watch him shift anxiously from one foot to the other. "Brittany!"

"Okay, fine. But I enjoy the anticipation." I ripped off the paper to reveal a black velvet box. Our eyes met, and I did wonder if an engagement ring awaited me, but I didn't think he'd present a marriage proposal so casually. I glanced up to ask in silence if it were okay for me to open the box.

"Yes!" He touched my elbow as if trying to hurry me along.

I held my breath and lifted the lid. My gorgeous broach stared back at me. "Is this the one from my shop, from the estate sale?" At his nod, I tilted my head. "How?"

"I missed you so much I drove to Seaview to spend Christmas Eve with you. But now you're here, and that's all that matters."

My jaw dropped open. "Wait, you drove to the beach to spend the holiday with me?"

He grinned. "Sure did."

"And I wasn't there, so you drove back in the same day?" I sat down on the couch, trying to process what he told me. "But how did you get the broach?"

"I stopped by your shop, and Nancy told me where you were. I saw the broach by the cash register and thought you deserved to have the piece for yourself." He grinned. "Like it?"

"Are you kidding?" I stared at the piece of jewelry, then at him, before I jumped up and wrapped my arms around his shoulders. "Thank you!"

"I knew you wanted it, but sales come first." He pulled me in his arms and bent down to kiss me. "Now it's yours."

His lips were so warm, tender, and loving. When we pulled apart, I said, "Thank you, so much. What a thoughtful gift. Time and again the broach tempted me to take it home." I leaned into his chest and wrapped my arms around him. "I love you."

"I love you too." He pulled away from the embrace and dropped to one knee, holding my hand as he awkwardly fished into his pants pocket to reveal a sparkling diamond ring. My mouth dropped open again. "I know we haven't known each other that long, but when you know, you know. Brittany, will you marry me?"

Tears flooded my eyes. I began to sob while smiling. "Of course, I will! I don't want to live life without you."

He slipped the ring onto my finger, and I sobbed happy tears of joy. I held out my hand, staring at the glittering ring. "I love you, Brittany."

Bo's wet tongue ran the length of my chin, as if giving us his blessing. I ran my hand down his back, giving him a scratch, and then turned to Chris.

I thrust myself into his arms, kissing him with all the passion I'd held deep inside my entire life. This was my fiancé, my man, the love of my life. "I love you too," I whispered through our kiss, not wanting to pull away from him.

After melting into his arms and holding each other for a time, Chris glanced at his watch. He pulled away quickly. "Everyone will be here in an hour! We have a lasagna to bake."

Reluctantly we left each other's arms and worked in the kitchen together as a team. Once he placed the lasagna in the oven and we had cleaned the kitchen, the doorbell rang. Ashley arrived first. She set bags of goodies on the freshly polished floor next to the door. We gave a round of hugs and said Merry Christmases.

"My mouth is watering. The lasagna smells divine, and now my belly is growling." Ashley rubbed her tummy for emphasis, and that's when she noticed my ring. She slapped her hand over her mouth, gasped dramatically, and then grabbed hold of my hand. "Excuse me, but do you both have something to tell me?"

I looked over my shoulder at Chris. "We sure do. We are engaged." Excitement at saying the words danced throughout my body. I never thought I'd say yes to marriage to a man who lived hours away from my shop, my home, and my family, not to mention to someone my parents had never met! Suddenly, I wanted to pick up the phone and call them.

Chris leaned in close to me. "And she said yes."

Ashley wrapped us in a hug and squealed.

"What's all the excitement about?" Susan asked as she stepped inside the house. She passed a covered dish to Ashley, who took it along with the salad bowl into the kitchen.

Chris spoke up, keeping me in one arm and hugging Susan with the other. "We are engaged."

It was Susan's turn to catch her breath. "Oh, goodness!" She kissed Chris's cheek, and then mine, pulling me into a warm, loving hug. "Congratulations. When is the wedding?"

"We just got engaged and haven't had time to discuss the details." My voice sounded giddy, and that was with me trying to reel in my excitement.

"Give us a chance," Chris said, laughing. "We've been engaged less than two hours."

Susan and I laughed. "Better get on that before she gets away." Susan's face brightened, and I knew she was happy for us.

Ashley hurried back into the room, likely not wanting to miss a single moment of excitement. "All things work out how they are meant to be. I'm glad you are moving to Snow Valley, and glad to have you close by, Cuz."

This was a moment where facing conflict had turned out well for me.

The timer went off in the kitchen, and Chris excused himself to tend to the lasagna. We followed, and the mood in Chris's house was light and festive.

Tim and Kat showed up right before dinner and we gave another round of hugs and cheer.

While we ate at the table, chatting about weddings, Christmas, and how well the Candlelight Tour had gone, I no longer missed my parents. I had the best family right here in this room. Sure, the addition of my parents would have been special, but I couldn't have asked for a better holiday gathering.

The day grew even better when we sat down to open presents. Susan untied a box from Chris that held the beautiful antique quilt we'd found in the servants' quarters, as well as a beautiful rose-colored candle that smelled like fresh-cooked cranberries from me. It was Chris's turn, and he held a present the size of a picture frame, wrapped in red foil paper with a silver bow.

"I can't wait for you to see this," Susan said, her voice sounding animated.

"I wonder what it is." He began to slowly unwrap the foil but stopped. "Heck, I'm going to rip it open like I never did as a kid." He tore the wrapping paper off in a flurry, revealing a frame as I'd guessed, but I wasn't able to see what was in the photo.

He paused, his face turning pale.

I wanted to lean in for a glance, but my intuition said to wait.

Chris looked up, pressing the frame against his chest. He raised his eyebrows in question at Susan.

"I've been holding onto the photo for a month. I found it at a thrift store." Susan grinned as Chris got up and walked over to her, pulling her into a hug while still holding onto the picture. "Thank you."

"What is it?" Ashley asked, leaning toward them as if prodding Chris to reveal the secret.

"It's a black and white photo of Amelia House." He turned the old photograph around so we could see. There was a large family in period clothing, smiling while standing in front of the house. "This is amazing. Thank you, Susan."

"My pleasure. When I saw it, I knew I had to buy it for you." She gleamed.

Chris squeezed her into a bigger hug, his voice shaking. "You're like the mom I never had."

Tears slid out of the corners of her eyes. "I'd love to be your unofficial adopted mom. I have no family and now I have you."

The scene unfolding in front of us warmed my heart. Both Chris and Susan's faces lit up like the tree lights.

We took turns studying the photo, and while everyone else seemed excited, I was ecstatic. "What an incredible glimpse back in time. And look how beautiful Amelia House was then. She still is."

Ashley poked me in the ribs. "Amelia House is meant for a family. How many kids do you want?"

Chris beamed and answered the question. "As many as possible." He wiggled his eyebrows and winked.

"That works for me." My face grew warm from everyone watching us.

Chris's face tightened, his gaze turning serious. "When I was a kid, I made a wish one Christmas morning. I asked for family and friends to spend the holiday with, wishing I could celebrate like other people, and here you all are."

"Wishes, my dear child, do come true," Susan said, holding her hands out to include all of us. "Never stop dreaming."

It was then that I remembered my own childhood dream to have a husband and kids of my own. Part of my wish came true today when Chris asked me to marry him, and it sounded as though he wanted children. I looked forward to carrying out my childhood family traditions with him, setting out cookies and milk for Santa on Christmas Eve, and opening gifts around the fire in front of the Christmas tree.

"Family hug," Ashley said, all of us standing to embrace each other in a circle of love. "We're all family and always will be."

Chris slid his arm around my lower back and pulled me close.

When I caught my breath from being squeezed in one big embrace, I leaned back to take it all in. "I think I can speak for Chris too, but even though my own parents aren't here for the holidays, this is the best Christmas I've ever had."

I gave my fiancé a kiss, and everyone clapped. It was much easier to learn to trust again after meeting the right man.

He looked up and said, "Merry Christmas, and a very happy new year."

Want to know when my next book is released? You will find out first. You'll also see my covers first and can often times help me choose. Join the fun and sign up for my e-mail list at LoriHayesAuthor.com

Dear Reader,

Thank you for reading my books! ☺ Without you, I wouldn't be an author. I love to write about a woman's journey, a couple's journey, family, and feral animals, so here's a treat! I have written a very special book to me that's endearing, emotional, and heartwarming. "Saving Nevada" is a novel based on a true story that will tug at your heartstrings and leave you cheering for the underdog. Join Haley on this captivating journey, where a wild mustang becomes not only her toughest challenge but also the catalyst for exploring love, self-discovery, and extraordinary strength found in the unlikeliest of friendships. If you love Heartland or The Black Stallion, you are in for a surprise!

If you haven't already read High Tide, the first book in the Crystal Coast Series, then take a relaxing vacation from home while sitting in your most comfy chair. Enjoy the beach but don't forget your sunglasses!
Thanks!
~~Lori~~

ABOUT THE AUTHOR

Lori Hayes lives in North Carolina with her family, horse, dog and overly affectionate cat. All of them are rescues except the children. Lori grew up in St. Louis, Missouri, which she loved, but moved to the coast because she treasures being close to the beach and mountains. If she had to pick one as a favorite, she'd choose the beach without a doubt, but the mountains are a close second. Family, photography, writing and horses are her passions. Please sign up for her newsletter by visiting her website at.
www.LoriHayesAuthor.com